# BELLA'S RODEO

## *Journey of a Thousand Miles 1*

**Alicia White**

**MENAGE AMOUR**

**Siren Publishing, Inc.**
**www.SirenPublishing.com**

**A SIREN PUBLISHING BOOK**
IMPRINT: Ménage Amour

BELLA'S RODEO


ISBN-10: 1-61926-641-5
ISBN-13: 978-1-61926-641-4

First Printing: February 2012

Cover design by Jinger Heaston


Printed in the U.S.A.

**PUBLISHER**
Siren Publishing, Inc.
www.SirenPublishing.com

# DEDICATION

This is for my wonderful husband, who has been supportive, every step of the way. He encourages my dreams of sexy cowboys.

To my best friend Erin, the sister of my heart. Thank you for always pushing me to do what I love. You are amazing and beautiful!

I hope that one day I'll be able to take a road trip just like Bella. I'm still looking for a town like this, as I'm sure most of the women in America are.

If anyone knows of a place similar to Coltmann County, let me know. I'll be the first one to drive us there.

# BELLA'S RODEO

***Journey of a Thousand Miles 1***

**ALICIA WHITE**



## Chapter 1

Isabella let out a long, quiet sigh as she packed up the single cardboard box that they gave to her to collect all her personal belongings. It was depressing to think of the last three years of her life as over. She graduated from college with high hopes of helping people in the community, but of course, being a nonprofit, the money just wasn't there to pay her salary. It seemed to be the same story for many people, but coming in this morning, she was not expecting to pack up and leave for good. As tears started to blur her vision, she moved faster. There was no way she was going to have a breakdown now.

"I've just got to get out of here, and then I can cry," Isabella said quietly to herself. "Don't lose it now. Just make it to the car."

Isabella kept trying to do some positive self-talk to help her complete her packing. Grabbing the last of her pictures, she headed for the door. Turning around and seeing her empty desk helped her to walk faster toward the exit and her boss that was waiting there for her.

"We're so sorry to see you go. We'll miss you." Kara leaned over and gave a half hug and a pat on the back. "Can I have your keys and also your name badge?"

The conversation probably sounded sincere to others who were listening, as if Isabella had decided to leave on her own. However, the smile was fake, and the good-bye was staged. Even the pat on the back was demeaning.

"Of course, thanks, it's been so great working here." Isabella decided to paint on a fake smile, stand straighter, and walk out with some dignity. She handed over her keys and name badge and walked out the door without a backward glance.

Isabella jumped into her car and threw the box on the floorboard. She grabbed her phone as she drove out of the parking lot. Even though she was a little sad still, she also had a feeling of relief. It was exciting to think of the next stages of her life and maybe doing something reckless. She decided to call her best friends and meet for a drink.

Jessica answered quickly. "Isabella…are you sick? You usually don't call this early in the morning."

Isabella shook her head and rolled her eyes. "No…I got laid off," she said with a sigh.

"Oh. My. God. Are you serious? I am so sorry. Where are you? Oh, forget it. Just drive over. I'll be waiting," Jessica said. She spoke so fast it was almost hard to keep up.

"All right, I'm on my way. Call Alyssa. We can all pretend it's five and start drinking," Isabella suggested with a smile, which actually sounded like the best idea she had ever had.

"Okay, come over. I'll call Alyssa. She can meet us here. See you soon. Drive safe," Jessica said and then hung up.

Isabella disconnected her phone and continued to drive, her mind in a complete frenzy. As she pulled up to Jessica's apartment, Alyssa was pulling up as well. She smiled to herself, grateful to have two amazing friends. It had always been this way with the three of them. Since high school, they had been inseparable, always dropping everything when there was an issue. Nothing seemed to be as important as their small family.

Isabella got out of her car and headed toward Alyssa, who was waiting by the front door. "Oh, Bella, I'm so sorry," she said as she pulled Isabella into a big hug.

Just then, Jessica opened the door. "Come in. I've got the shot glasses lined up," she said with a smile.

The three friends headed straight to the bar area. Jessica had a great apartment. The whole thing had been completely gutted and modernized. The kitchen had a beautiful marble countertop that jutted into the dining room, providing a great bar area. True to her word, there were three shot glasses, already filled, lime wedges, and of course, a full bottle of tequila. This was going to be a great afternoon, Bella thought with a smile.

"So, I'll give the first toast to start us off," Jessica said as she handed out the glasses and grabbed her own. "To great friends, fresh starts, and a new door opening," she held up her shot glass. They smiled at each other and downed their shots.

"Wow, I don't know how you two can drink this stuff," Alyssa said with a wince as she put her glass down. "So, tell us what happened, Bella."

Bella cringed a bit and started pouring. She just wanted to run away for a while and not think.

"I don't really want to talk about it. I've complained to you guys for a few months now. It's just politics. I wanted to do more to help the kids, and I couldn't. It's for the best, and I just don't want to keep talking about it. What I do want to do is go on that road trip we've been talking about," Bella said with a smile.

They had been talking about driving across the United States since graduating high school. Living in California all their lives, they all dreamed about seeing the country and having an adventure. Something always came up—college, job, family obligations—and there just never seemed to be any time.

"Seriously..." Jessica said as she looked over at Alyssa. "We've talked about it quite a bit, and I really wish I could, but I have too much going on. You know I've been selling my designs online. I can't fill orders while I'm on the road. What about you, Alyssa?"

Alyssa had a look on her face that couldn't be deciphered easily. Finally, she said, "Actually, the semester is over. I finished my last final a couple days ago. I wasn't sure if I should look for a summer job. This might be the perfect opportunity."

Bella was so excited she jumped up and hugged Alyssa. "Thank you, I really need this. I need to run away for a while and have no responsibilities," Bella whispered. She hadn't realized she was holding her breath until she spoke.

"When are you thinking about leaving town? Where will you head? There needs to be planning before a trip like this. You can't just pack and bag and leave," Jessica said, irritated that her friends were actually thinking of doing this without her.

"I think that's the best idea. No map, no real direction, just heading out on the road. We would leave and go through Arizona, New Mexico, Texas, and head for Florida. We could plan to be gone the whole summer," Bella said with so much excitement, she was pacing and thinking of all the sights they could see.

Alyssa got up and started walking around as well. "When should we go? This is going to be great. I'm so excited, I want to go home and pack now."

"I can't believe you two are actually thinking about this. It's a horrible idea. Bella, you're upset, but it will pass. You'll be fine. Don't make a rash decision because you're feeling depressed," Jessica said.

"I'm not. We've been talking about this for so long. This is the best time. We want you to come, but if you can't, then Alyssa and I will go. We can head out in a couple of days. That will give us time to tell everyone, get some maps, and pack up," Bella told them. This was the perfect time to get on the road and drive. Bella grabbed her purse, forgetting the shot glass on the counter. "Well, I'm feeling better. This is going to be great. Alyssa, head home and get packing. I'll get some maps together and pack as well. We can head out on Monday morning. That will give us a couple of days."

Bella turned toward Jessica and hoped she could convince her to join them. "Please, Jessica, you can bring your laptop and still work. Put the shipping on hold, or better yet, actually let your assistant work for you."

Bella took a deep breath and made her best puppy face at Jessica, hoping to convince her. Jessica was always such a control freak. She had an assistant who just sat around waiting for work to do. Jessica wouldn't let anyone do anything. She had to be the boss at all times. She was strong and independent, and she didn't have any family but Bella and Alyssa.

Jessica frowned. "I can't, but I do want you two to go and have fun, though. Send me lots of pictures. I love you both. Promise to drive safe and to call me at least daily to tell me where you are. Jeez, this is a bad idea. Just stay safe, and use your heads," Jessica said in her motherly voice. She was always mothering them.

"Okay, well, I'm going to head home. Thanks, guys. I love you both, and I'm so lucky to have great friends like you," Bella said, smiling at her friends. She gave both Jessica and Alyssa a hug and then headed toward her car and home.

The weekend went by quickly, and in a blur, Bella packed a couple bags with all her favorite clothes and shoes, cleaned her house, and made sure to empty the fridge. She also chatted with Jessica and Alyssa, begging Jessica to come and making sure Alyssa packed many different outfits.

On Monday morning, Bella drove over to Alyssa's to pick her up. Alyssa walked out of her house with a huge smile, and her bags trailing behind her. This was it, their great adventure, just the two of them. As Alyssa loaded her bags in the back of Bella's Nissan Cube, they saw Jessica speed around the corner and head toward them.

"Do you think she's here to stop us, or say good-bye?" Alyssa asked.

Bella just shook her head. Jessica was very persistent, so her money was on stopping them, but she didn't voice it.

Jessica got out of her car and headed over. She was wearing her pink Juicy Couture jogging suit and had a coffee in her hand. "So, you two really going to do this?" she asked, looking between Bella and Alyssa.

"Yeah, are you here to stop us or join us?" Bella asked with a challenge in her voice.

"Well…I've decided to join you, but I'm driving, and I have the maps all highlighted of where we're going," she stated.

Bella and Alyssa looked at each other, hiding their grins. This was so like Jessica. She just had to be in charge. Luckily, it didn't bother either of them. As Jessica turned and headed back to her car, Bella and Alyssa unloaded their luggage and headed toward Jessica's small SUV.

With the luggage all loaded, the three friends headed out of town in search of an adventure.

# Chapter 2

They were in the middle of nowhere. The car was fuming, a horrible burning smell, and they were pushing it just to make it to a gas station. The trip had been great up to this point. They had taken the 15 north out of California and gotten onto Highway 40 heading east. They drove through Arizona, making a few stops, and then through New Mexico. They were now in Texas, somewhere between Amarillo and the Oklahoma state line. They had just hit the Coltmann County line, and so far, they had not seen anything. They were so far off the beaten path, and the car was starting to choke and jerk. Jessica quickly pulled the car to the side of the road. It made a horrible sound and completely stopped.

"Holy shit! I can't believe this. We are so screwed," Jessica said, hitting her head on the steering wheel. She kept at it, hitting her head repeatedly.

They were all silent and in shock. Bella had no idea where they were, and she knew that Jessica and Alyssa were just as clueless. Of course, to top it all off, no cell service, so no hope of calling for help.

Finally, Bella broke the silence. "Okay, let's grab our bags and continue to head down this road. We should eventually find someone who can help us."

They all started getting out of the small SUV. Each grabbed her own luggage and headed down the street.

Luckily, the sun was going down, and the summer heat was slowly easing. It was still about a hundred degrees outside, but at least it was a dry heat. They had only been walking for about twenty minutes. Sweat slowly started to trickle down Bella's back, her feet were aching, and her body hurt. Did she have to pack so much? These suitcases were excessively heavy. If she just left them on the side of the road and kept walking, could they be picked up later, or would they be stolen? Did she actually care anymore? This sucked. These questions kept going through her mind. They finally turned a corner in the road and spotted a building in the distance.

"Oh, thank God. I seriously didn't think we would find anything out here," Alyssa said with a sigh and shake of her head. She was covered in sweat.

As they walked closer, the town got bigger. People were walking around, holding hands, smiling. This seemed like a nice place. The gas station was the first building they walked up to, and luckily, attached was a mechanic shop. They would be back on the road in no time.

"Austin Brothers' Shop," Jessica said. "Okay, I'll go in. Maybe they have a tow truck. Drop the luggage and wait here."

Jessica headed into the shop, and Bella and Alyssa literally collapsed on top of their luggage.

* * * *

Jessica was dripping with sweat. She was tired, cranky, and in desperate need of a shower, water, and food. The order did not matter, as long as it happened soon. This whole issue with her car was definitely pissing her off. They were off schedule and off the damn highway. She didn't even know what had caused her to pull off the main highway and go toward this small town. Maybe it was a gut instinct. Either way, they were here, and her car was broken down. Where was "here"?

"Hello…excuse me…my car broke down, and I need some help," Jessica called out into the shop. She didn't see anyone, so she started looking around. "Excuse me, anyone here?"

Finally, a man came through the side door of the shop. He had a cowboy hat on, and Jessica couldn't quite make out his face. He was about six and a half feet tall and had huge shoulders. Most men would be jealous. He looked like some sort of old-time warrior. He wore jeans and a white T-shirt and had a pair of cowboy boots on. Then he looked up and stared right into her eyes. Wow, he was magnificent. He had the most amazing blue eyes she had ever seen, so incredibly deep. His hair was long, black, and curly, from what she could see. She wanted to knock the hat off and push her fingers through it. He was the type of man who would look amazing in a suit or just walking around in, well, nothing. He was without a doubt, absolutely gorgeous.

His lips, she wanted them all over her body. Starting at her feet and moving up until they reached her lips. His lips were moving, but she could not understand him. She felt like she was in some sort of a trance. She could see everything, in slow motion, but she couldn't hear anything but her own heartbeat.

"Ma'am, are you all right?" he said with concern. He walked over and smiled down at her. Lifting his fingers, he gently caressed Jessica's cheek and tipped her chin up. She hadn't realized that her mouth was hanging open. "Ma'am, can I help you?"

"Oh…y–yes…I'm sorry. My car broke down, and my friends and I have been walking for quite a while. I'm just exhausted. Do you have a tow truck? Can you fix my car?" Jessica asked.

She was talking fast. She was tired, but more importantly, she had just been caught ogling this man. She was soaking wet, and it wasn't just from the long walk and the hot weather. Her nipples were tight, and she could barely breathe. Jessica wanted to throw herself in his arms. That had never happened before. Her body's reactions were foreign. When it came to men and sex, she was the boss. She told them when, where, and how. She needed to stay far away from this man and keep her guard up. She could tell already that he would be dangerous to her heart.

* * * *

Chase looked at the beautiful little pixie face and knew she was the one for him and his brother, Beau. He felt it soul deep. She took his breath away and revived him all in the same moment. She was five foot five with gorgeous long, curly blonde hair and light hazel eyes. She looked like an absolute angel. It was his lucky day. She also looked exhausted and in need of some food. She was a little on the skinny side for his taste but still so damn perfect. She was staring at him as if she wanted to lick him and run away all at the same time. She kept looking him up and down and seemed interested, but then she would shake her head. It almost seemed like she was talking herself out of wanting him. That would not do.

"Yes, ma'am, I have a tow truck. I can take you out and get your car, then bring it back here. My brother should be back soon. He just went to the café across the street to grab some supper. Why don't we join him? He'd love to meet you, princess," Chase said in his slow Texas drawl and added a little smile and wink at the end, hoping she would. He could not wait for Beau to see her. If Beau's reaction was anything like his, they were done for. He was already sporting an erection he hoped she didn't notice. He didn't want to scare her away. She was skittish. He could tell from the look in her eyes he was making her nervous.

Finally, after a few moments, she looked up. "Yeah, that sounds fine. My friends are waiting outside."

She led him outside to where two women were lying on their luggage under a tree. They were obviously exhausted, as well. He wondered what would bring three women to Coltmann County then realized it didn't matter. He and his brother had their work cut for them if they were going to keep this little princess occupied and interested.

* * * *

Bella saw Jessica come out of the garage with a sexy man following her. Her first thought was, *Wow, I hope there are more men like him here.* She automatically turned to Alyssa, wondering if she saw him as well. From the look in her eyes, it was obvious she was thinking the same thing. *Damn, hot cowboy.*

Bella and Alyssa both started to stand and gather their things as Jessica approached with the sexy cowboy. She came over and announced, "Hey guys, they have a tow truck. And he—I'm sorry, I don't know your name." Jessica stopped to look at the sexy cowboy.

He smiled down at her and, in the most amazing accent Bella had ever heard, said, "I'm Chase, Chase Austin. My brother and I own this shop. Nice to meet you, ladies." He tipped his cowboy hat and smiled. She felt her knees weaken a little just from listening to him, he had a deep voice and a thick accent.

Bella recovered first and stepped forward. "Hello, I'm Bella Williams, this is Alyssa Fredricks, and you've already talked to Jessica Beckett."

He nodded again. "I was just telling Jess that we should go to the café across the street and have some supper with my brother, Beau. Then I can go pick up your car. There is a small motel here in town where you ladies can stay for as long as you'd like."

"Thanks, but we aren't staying too long, just long enough to get my car fixed. We can book a room for the night. In fact, Alyssa, can you head to the motel and book us a room, then meet us at the café? The sooner we get my car here, the sooner it can get fixed," Jessica said. She looked a little shocked that he'd called her Jess, as if they were old friends or lovers. She recovered quickly and was her in-charge, normal self again the next moment.

Alyssa nodded and started gathering her luggage. They watched as she headed across the street, toward the motel.

Jessica turned toward Chase. "Lead the way to the café. We're starved."

Chase started to gather all the rest of the luggage. Bella let him take everything. She was tired and had no problem with him flexing his muscles.

"Chase, I can carry my own luggage, you know," Jessica told him. Her voice sounded irritated, and with her hand on her hips and the serious look on her face, Bella found herself cringing a little.

Bella quickly interjected, knowing Jessica was getting irritated with the help and attention. In fact, Jessica was more annoyed than usual. "Jess, let him carry the bags. He's just being polite. It's a Southern gentleman thing," she said. Bella grabbed Jessica's arm and started to follow behind Chase, glad she had intervened. She knew there was more Jessica wanted to say, but she allowed herself to be pulled as they went toward the café.

As they walked down the sidewalk of the small town, Bella noticed all the different shops. The town really had an old Western, homey feel to it. There was a nice breeze and a very peaceful atmosphere. There were even a few couples walking around, and she noticed that some of the women were holding hands with multiple men. Bella blinked and really tried to focus on what she was seeing just in case her overactive imagination was playing tricks on her. Then she slowly started to smile. This was going to be one hell of a vacation. She looked over at Jessica to see if she noticed as well, and then realized that she was staring at Chase as he walked ahead of them. This was becoming very interesting indeed.

# Chapter 3

Chase held open the door as Bella and Jessica walked into the café. They walked, in and Bella noticed right away that the little café was quite homey. The walls were a pale yellow, and there was a large tree painted on one wall, with birds flying. The colors were so vivid. There were also other murals painted throughout the small building adding unique character to the café. There were quite a few booths where people chatted quietly. There was also a low counter with stools. The overall appearance reminded Bella of a '50s style diner, although everything was modern and simple. The feeling of the overall place was what drew her. It was somewhere she always wanted to live.

It was a personal place, where people actually knew each other and cared about each other. Some of the people stopped their conversations and looked their way. Bella smiled as she held on to Jessica's arm.

One man in a back booth stood and started to walk toward them. He looked almost exactly like Chase. This had to be Chase's brother, Bella thought with a smile. As the man got closer, Bella noticed that Jessica got tenser. She stood straighter and stared at the approaching stranger. Bella smiled knowingly. Things were just getting better and better. She shook her head and tried not to laugh aloud at the scene unfolding.

"Hey, Chase, who are these lovely ladies?" the man asked.

"I'd like to introduce you to Jess and Bella. Ladies, this is my older brother, Beau," Chase replied with a smile.

Bella stepped forward and shook his hand but noticed that he seemed to have eyes only for Jessica, just like Chase. She wondered if these two men were into sharing or if they were planning to fight it out over her friend. Every minute spent here, Bella was finding to be more entertaining than the last. This was so great. She planned to watch Jessica and these men to see if anything developed.

"Nice to meet you. Are you ladies hungry? I just ordered. Why don't you join me?" Beau asked with genuine interest.

"That's a great idea. They have a third joining soon, Alyssa, another friend traveling with them," Chase told his brother as he followed him back to the table. Bella and Jessica followed along after them.

Just as they sat down, the server headed over. She was a bit older than they were, probably in her early fifties. She had a bright smile, and her nametag read "Susan."

"Good evening, Chase, Beau. Who are your new friends? There are a few other men that are quite curious." The server looked over at a couple of the tables, where groups of men were sitting, enjoying their dinner. She smiled and looked back, facing Jessica and Bella. "You know small towns. Everyone always wants to know everyone else's business. By the way, I'm Susan."

Bella smiled and peeked over at the tables. It seemed this town was full of sexy men. "I'm Bella, this is my friend Jessica, and our other friend will be here shortly, Alyssa. Our car broke down, so we'll be here until it's fixed, staying at the motel." Bella quickly realized she said too much and stopped herself from saying more, receiving a scowl from Jessica.

* * * *

Beau and Chase laughed softly as they looked at the beautiful women in front of them. Jessica seemed to be a bit on the quieter side, while Bella talked up a storm. More women were exactly what this town needed. Already, the men outnumbered the women five to one.

It wasn't uncommon for brothers, or even friends, to share a woman. From the looks these women were getting, the men were definitely interested. They would have to tell them that Jessica wasn't available. They were already feeling quite possessive and protective when it came to her. It was a strange feeling, but at the same time, they recognized her as theirs.

"So, ladies, what brings you to Coltmann County?" Beau asked, genuinely curious as to what had brought these women here.

"Well, I lost my job a couple weeks ago, and we decided to go on a little adventure. We've been talking about a road trip for years, and this was the right time. Unfortunately, our car broke down, and here we are," Bella answered for them both. Yep, Bella was the more talkative of the two.

Beau wasn't sure if Jessica was shy or if she was purposely not talking. She seemed to be interested, though. She was staring at both him and Chase with longing and fear in her eyes. He wanted to pull her into his lap and comfort her, tell her he would protect her. She seemed fragile one minute, then tough the next. She was a puzzle that he desperately wanted to solve. He looked over at Chase and noticed the same longing in his eyes. They needed to come up with a plan as to how to win her over. They could pick up her car and then start there.

* * * *

Just then, the door opened, and Alyssa walked in. She smiled when she saw them, and walked over. "This town is amazing. I love it. Have you noticed all the hot men?" she said, staring at Bella and Jessica.

Finally, after a pause, Beau and Chase laughed aloud. Alyssa actually blushed a little, not realizing how loud she had been talking. Alyssa quickly grabbed a chair and pulled it up to the booth to sit down.

"Alyssa, we were waiting on you to order. Did you get us a nice room?" Jessica asked, trying to change the subject.

"Yeah, I got us three separate rooms, actually, since they were fairly inexpensive. The motel is practically empty, so the owners gave me an excellent rate. I thought we could all use the privacy after being cooped up for a while," Alyssa explained.

"That's perfect. Thanks, Alyssa," Jessica said with a smile. The server walked over then, and they all ordered.

"I'll have a burger, fries, and a Coke," Bella said.

Her friends nodded in agreement. It seemed that they were all starving after not eating since having a granola bar for breakfast. They all sat in a comfortable silence, finally feeling relaxed after the stressful events. The server brought over their food, and they all quickly dove in, inhaling everything.

"How long do you think it will take to fix my car?" Jessica asked, breaking the silence.

"Well, Chase and I can drive the truck to go pick it up tonight, and then we'll check it out first thing in the morning. Why don't you come over when you've had a good night's sleep and some breakfast? I'm sure we'll have some answers for you then," Beau answered.

"Thanks. I'm ready to drop, I'm so tired," Jessica said with a yawn. She was feeling stressed and cranky.

* * * *

Bella was looking around while she ate. She couldn't help it. There was some amazing eye candy around here, and she didn't want to miss the view. As Jessica, Chase, and Beau talked comfortably about the drive and the town, Bella stared at the table across from them, where three men were sitting, talking quietly. Every few minutes they looked over, and she would quickly look away.

*What do they feed the men here?* They were all tall, sexy, and built. Every woman in America would want to be here if they knew this place existed. Bella sent a silent prayer that they would be stuck here for a while. She smiled and shook her head. God probably didn't answer those sorts of prayers.

Jessica's gasp drew Bella from her thoughts, and she turned to see Jessica with her mouth slightly open and her eyes wide, staring at Beau and Chase. "What?" Bella asked. Obviously, she'd missed part of the conversation.

Jessica turned and said, "Did you hear that? They just said that most men in this town share a woman, as in there are multiple men married to a single woman." As if she needed to rephrase it more for Bella to understand.

Bella smiled and nodded. "I know."

"What do you mean, you know?" Jessica asked quickly.

"Just look around, the people sitting at the tables, the couples walking around the town. You would've noticed if you weren't staring at Chase's ass on the way in here," Bella explained.

Again, Beau and Chase laughed aloud. "You are too precious, Bella. Seriously, I hope you meet some men here that can keep up with you," Chase said as he shook his head knowingly and winked at her.

Just then, three men walked up to the table. They were huge up close. When they were sitting down, they looked to be about six feet tall. Looking up now to meet their gazes, Bella noticed they were much bigger. They were all amazing up close. They had brown hair, slightly different shades, and deep brown eyes. They were wearing jeans, boots, and T-shirts and held their hats. Bella could not help herself. She looked them up and down. Finally, she landed and stared at the obvious bulges in their jeans. *They must be huge all over,* she thought as she looked back to their eyes. It was obvious from their smiles that they saw her staring at their crotches. Good thing she wasn't shy.

They were yummy. Bella was breathing a little heavier, and thoughts of the three of them together came rushing into her mind.

The things she was willing to do almost scared her since she really didn't have that much experience with men to begin with. Her nipples tightened, and she felt moisture beginning to flow onto her panties. All of a sudden, she was becoming uncomfortable, and started to squirm on the booth bench.

"Hey, guys, I see you wanted to come over and meet the ladies," Chase said with a smile.

"Hello. Yeah, we did. We saw you two surrounded by beautiful women and thought we might be able to take one off your hands," he answered with a wink. "I'm Clint, and these are my brothers, Cody and Clay Colton. We own the Triple C Ranch, about twenty miles outside of town. I would love to give you a personal tour, beautiful," Clint said to Bella.

The way he looked at her, and spoke to her, made her feel owned. This was the type of man she craved. He was totally alpha, secure, and staring at her as if he were starving. She felt beautiful and petite in comparison to their larger bodies, their hard, wide shoulders, and muscular arms.

* * * *

Chase smiled at his friends, having known exactly what they were thinking before they walked over to introduce themselves to Bella. She was a cute thing.

Chase introduced the beautiful women. "This is Bella Williams, Jessica Beckett, and Alyssa Fredricks." He knew they only really cared about meeting Bella, especially since they were all staring at her. "We were just heading out to pick up Jessica's car and walk the ladies to the motel where they're staying."

The Colton brothers had been looking for a woman they could call their own for a while. From the looks on their faces, Bella was the one. Chase smiled to himself. This day couldn't have been more perfect. The thing about having a ménage relationship was that everyone had to agree, especially the brothers or friends. The men needed to be on the same page, needed to have an understanding of each other's needs before introducing a woman into the equation.

* * * *

Clay stepped forward and offered Bella his arm. "Ma'am, I'd be honored to escort you to the motel," he said with an innocent smile.

Bella reached for his arm, and he gently pulled her from the booth. She felt a sizzle of heat run up her arm at the contact. She knew he felt it, too, by the way his eyes widened. He held on to her hand when she tried to pull it from his arm. Bella tried to control her breathing as her heart pounded in her chest.

"Thank you," Bella said quietly. She had no idea what else to say. These feelings and thoughts were so new to her. She didn't want to say anything too soon. They weren't going to be in town long enough for real feelings to form. At that thought, disappointment consumed her. She had felt a definite spark. How often did things like that happen? So far, it had never happened to her.

* * * *

Cody and Clint stepped forward at the obvious pain on her face. Clint tipped her chin up so that she was looking into his chocolate-brown eyes. He smiled gently down at her. "Bella, are you all right? Is it okay if we walk you to the motel?" He was trying to talk softly since he could see the sadness in her eyes and didn't want to scare her away. They were big men, after all, and she was just a tiny little thing.

She smiled then, although the smile didn't quite meet her eyes. "Yeah, that's fine. Thanks."

Clint nodded his head and looked toward Cody. Cody took her other arm, and the four of them walked out of the café and toward the motel, knowing that Beau and Chase would escort her friends.

They had dinner at the café only a few days a week. It was amazing to be having supper and to see this gorgeous, petite woman walk in the door. She was so beautiful, with short, straight black hair and small bangs that were in a perfect line above her eyebrows. She had creamy light-brown skin and a perfect complexion. When she talked or laughed across the café, it was like listening to music. She also had the most unbelievable curves. She might be considered "thick" to some people, but to him and his brothers, she was perfect. Her breasts were a handful, and it was easy to see she had a waist that flared out and turned into her hips, giving her an hourglass figure. Her ass was amazing, and as she walked, there was a very subtle sway. Clint couldn't take his eyes off her. His attention divided between his brothers' looks of contentment and the temptress they had been lucky to find.

* * * *

As they walked closer to the motel, Bella wasn't sure how to say good night. Would she see these men again? From the looks on their faces, she decided not to doubt herself. She became bold and found herself gently rubbing her fingers on Cody and Clay's arms. Occasionally she would turn her head to see Clint watching her.

"Thank you for walking me to the motel. I need to wait for Alyssa to get here. I forgot to get my room key from her," Bella explained.

Clay smiled down at her and said, "Don't worry, sweetheart. Alyssa gave me your room key as we headed out the door. Looks like you're room number ten."

She hadn't even noticed where the rest of the group had gone. She had been so immersed in Clint, Cody, and Clay. She hadn't been paying attention at all.

"Oh, I didn't even notice." She smiled at them.

"You don't have to worry about anything from now on. If you'll let us, we'd consider it an honor to always take care of you," Clay said.

It was obvious from his tone that he was sincere, and looking into his eyes, she wanted to let them take care of her. However, she remembered that her visit here was going to be short, and she really couldn't afford to be emotionally attached. Even though, deep down, she wanted to. She wanted nothing more than to invite these beautiful men into her motel room, but she knew if she did, when they left—not if they left—she would be heartbroken. Already, she felt close to them in a way she couldn't understand.

"Thank you for walking me here. I guess I'd better go in, take a shower, and go to bed. I'm so tired," she explained.

"Absolutely, beautiful," Cody said. "Would you consider coming out to our ranch tomorrow? We can come here and pick you up in the morning."

"Sure, that would be great. I've never been on a ranch before. I love to go horseback riding. Do you have horses?" she asked. She didn't know what kind of ranch they had.

"Yeah, horses, cows, bulls, all the barn animals," Clint said with a laugh in his voice.

He had the most amazing voice. Just listening to him, she became wet. If she stayed outside her room and talked any longer, she would just start to get weaker and invite them in. So instead, she said, "Good night, I'll see you tomorrow then."

Clint pulled Bella close, holding her securely in his arms. He leaned down slowly, giving her plenty of time to pull back or push him away. She moved closer still, their bodies completely touching. She stood up on her toes to get closer, and when their mouths touched, it felt like coming home. The kiss slowly became more intense. He slipped his tongue into her mouth. He tasted amazing, like sin, and he played with her tongue, convincing her to join in.

"Beautiful." She barely heard the whispered voice of Cody.

"She's amazing," Clay answered back.

As the kiss slowly ended, Cody stepped up and pulled her to his body. He swept his mouth down to devour her. He kissed so differently than Clint. Where Clint was playful and gentle, Cody ate at her mouth like a starving man.

Bella was barely able to breathe when Cody pulled away and Clay slowly pulled her to his body. He rubbed her back and let his hand slowly run down and massage her bottom. He leaned down and kissed her with such reverence it brought tears to her eyes. All three of these men were so overwhelming. She wanted more.

When the kissed ended, she smiled at them, gathered her wits, and walked into her hotel room. Before she shut the door, she turned. "Good night, I'll see you tomorrow."

All three of the men stood in a row, with huge smiles on their faces. "Good night, baby, I'll be here to pick you up around ten," Clint said.

Bella turned and shut the door. She leaned against it and listened to them walking away.

Oh my God, her mouth still tingled from the scorching kisses. Bella locked the door and headed to the bathroom. Looking around, she spotted her luggage. How had she not realized they brought her things to the motel? She shook her head. She had been so focused on them she hadn't seen them grab her things.

She quickly started undressing and getting things organized, and then started the shower. She climbed in under the hot water and just let it run down over her. This whole day had been crazy, and now she had just met the most wonderful men. Should she go for it and have some fun while they were here? Should she tell them the kiss was wrong and keep herself at a distance? In all of her thirty-one years, nothing like this had ever happened before.

* * * *

After she got out of the shower, she felt a lot better, almost energized. She was dressed, and sat in one of the large overstuffed chairs, thinking about how they had ended up in such an amazing place. Bella didn't feel tired any longer. Meeting Clint, Clay, and Cody had been like a wet, dirty dream come true. They were magnificent, and she wanted them. Maybe she could have a little fun before leaving town.

She had been sitting in silence for a while, when someone knocked at her motel room door. She walked over to the door and asked, "Who is it?"

"Hey, Bella, it's me, Alyssa," was the immediate response.

Bella opened her door to see Alyssa, all showered and dressed, wearing a pair of jeans, a cute top, and of course, her gorgeous Steve Madden pumps.

"All dressed up and nowhere to go?" Bella asked with a smile.

"I can't sleep. I took a shower and decided to get dressed. I heard there was a pub down the street. Do you want to go?" Alyssa asked. She was dressed to kill, that was for sure.

Alyssa had always been outspoken and adventurous. That's what drew Bella to her in high school. She was beautiful, although not in the skinny model way. Alyssa was five foot eight and had obvious curves. She was a size twelve or fourteen. Her hair was brown and cut to her shoulders, with a slight curl, and she had the most beautiful green eyes. Men were always looking at her, but for some reason, Alyssa was single, almost as if she didn't believe that the men found her attractive.

"Sure, just give me a few minutes to change, and I'll go with you. I was feeling the same way. Restless. Do you think we should ask Jessica to join us?" Bella asked.

"No, she really was tired. I think she's out for the night. Go ahead and get ready. I'll wait here," Alyssa answered.

Bella quickly started to get ready. She grabbed a pair of jeans, a tank top, and a pair of strappy heels. Part of Bella was hoping she might see Clint, Clay, and Cody, while the other part was praying that they wouldn't be at the pub.

Bella and Alyssa walked out of the motel and down the street, toward the pub. It wasn't a far walk, the night was warm, and there were still a few people walking around. When they got to the door, the place was busy, and it seemed to be karaoke night. They both looked at each other and smiled. This was going to be fun.

# Chapter 4

As they walked into the pub, it was like a picture from Ireland. Everything was so beautiful. The whole bar was made of dark oak. The mirror on the back wall clearly reflected all the bottles in front of it. The bold name of the bar, Spread Eagle, painted over the glass was crisp, yet faded, as if it had been there for years. Looking around, Bella could tell this place was loved by its owner and well used by the patrons. The wood had a deep grain that had been smoothed over the years by the many customers.

Bella laughed aloud when she read the name again. Holy cow. She just realized it was dirty. The owners obviously had a sense of humor. She was impressed with this pub. Bella and Alyssa went and sat at the bar. Although the place was busy, there were still open seats.

The bartender walked over, smiling at them broadly. "Good evening, ladies, what can I get you?"

Alyssa quickly answered, obviously ready for some serious drinking, "Can we get two shots of tequila and a couple of beers? Whatever you have on tap's fine."

The bartender gave a nod and started grabbing some glasses. "So, are you ladies visiting, or are you moving here?" He tried to make casual conversation, although he did seem a bit nervous.

"We're just passing through. Our car broke down, so I guess we're here until it gets fixed," Alyssa told him.

"I'm sorry to hear that. I'm Justin Truman, and my partner over there"—he nodded his head toward the other side of the bar—"is Grant Hollis."

"Nice to meet you. I'm Alyssa Fredricks, and this is my friend

Bella Williams." Bella looked around while Justin got their drinks together and chatted with Alyssa. They seemed to have made a quick connection. It was nice to see Alyssa flirting a little bit. Justin was a nice-looking man, not as hot as the Colton brothers, but still cute. He had dirty-blond hair that touched the collar of his shirt, and blue eyes. He seemed sweet, and Alyssa deserved sweet.

The drinks arrived, and Bella threw back her shot and asked Justin for another. Today had been so crazy, and she just felt like winding down so she could go to sleep. A singer finally went up to the stage, after getting some coaxing from his friends, and started to sing Garth Brooke's "The Dance." It was such a sweet song. Bella felt tears sting her eyes. She could only shake her head and blame it on exhaustion. She slammed back her second shot and looked over to see Alyssa looking at her with concern.

"I thought I might sing tonight, if they have any music by Adele here," Bella told her, hoping that Alyssa wouldn't ask any questions. Usually when it came to karaoke, she never got onstage. "Don't look at me like that. Nobody knows me, and besides, we're probably leaving tomorrow."

Justin walked over with the binder of music selections and put it down in front of them. Bella picked it up and flipped through it until she found the song she was looking for. She wrote it down and handed it to Justin.

Bella sipped her beer, waiting for her turn. She was starting to get scared as a few more people went up onstage. When she was about to chicken out, she heard her name being called over the microphone. Alyssa looked at her with a raised eyebrow, as if in challenge, so Bella got up and walked to the stage.

The music started to play, and Bella took a deep breath and started to sing along to Adele's "Rolling in the Deep." She felt confident and powerful and sang her heart out. Bella smiled over at Alyssa, who was staring at her in utter shock, although she was clapping along and swaying. As the song was ending, Bella looked toward the corner of the bar and saw the three beautiful men she had been hoping, yet dreading, to see. They were all looking at her with intense eyes, and she wasn't at all sure what would happen when she got off the stage.

Bella bowed to a standing ovation. Never in her life had something like that happened. As she walked off the stage, the next singer walked on. She walked toward the bar and the third shot glass calling her name. She downed it as she faced Alyssa, knowing that the Colton brothers were walking toward her.

"So, Alyssa, it's your turn. What are you gonna sing?" Bella asked, already starting to slur her words. Jeez, what a lightweight, she was already feeling buzzed.

"It's a surprise, just for you. I think I'm up next," Alyssa told her.

"Alyssa…I was just wondering, can you tell me when the Colton brothers are behind me? I saw them sitting in the back," Bella whispered loudly.

"We're right here, sweetheart," came a voice from behind her, and she knew it was Clint.

"I thought you were tired. Couldn't sleep?" asked Cody.

"No, I was too restless after you left, and Alyssa asked me to join her for a drink," Bella explained. She turned around and was immediately surrounded by their warmth and clean, earthy smell. She inhaled deeply, trying to memorize their unique scent.

"You have such a beautiful singing voice, baby. It's almost like you should be in one of those fancy jazz bars," Clay explained.

"Thank you," Bella said, not realizing that their praise really was important to her. "Alyssa is going up now. Do you guys want to sit down and watch with me?" Bella asked, wanting to still be surrounded by them.

Alyssa walked onstage, and Bella smiled. Alyssa loved to sing. She was always signing up, especially on karaoke night at their favorite place in San Diego. The song started, and Alyssa started to sing Train's "Marry Me." Bella started to laugh. This night was getting weirder. She didn't want to look at the brothers. It was not a song she could really enjoy while surrounded by them.

Clint stood up and walked in front of Bella, holding his hand out in an invitation to dance. Bella looked up at him, gave a half smile, and stood up. They walked to the dance floor hand in hand, and Clint pulled her close to his chest and started to sway slowly. Bella held on to the front of his shirt as he surrounded her with his massive body. She laid her head on his chest and closed her eyes. She felt his lips kiss the top of her head, and this time she smiled and even felt herself tearing up a bit. This was the perfect song, after all.

As the song ended, she took a deep breath and held his shirt a little tighter. The last thing she wanted to do was let go of him. She tried to memorize his scent and the feel of his chest against her face. Sadness engulfed her. She tried to rein in her emotions, but after today, and really, the past month, she couldn't stop the tears from coming. Before she could do anything, she was sobbing quietly in Clint's shirt. She was crying for the loss of the job she loved, she was crying for finding these men in Texas and not at home in California, and she was crying because she was so darn tired.

* * * *

Clint held her tight knowing that she was crying and trying to give her some privacy from the other patrons in the pub. He looked over at his brothers and nodded for them to come over. They really should all be comforting her.

After they had left her motel room, they walked back to his truck that was parked out in front of the café. He had decided to bring his brothers to the pub so they could talk about their plans for seducing the beautiful Bella.

After sitting in the far corner booth and coming up with a few different scenarios for when they got her to their ranch tomorrow, they looked up to see her walking into the bar with her friend close by her side. At first, they had wanted to jump up and go talk to her, but

Clint had his brothers stay seated to see if she would notice them. He also wanted to see her interact with the other people, to see if she would flirt with any other men. She looked a bit sad. Though she was smiling, her face didn't light up, and he knew she wasn't really happy.

When she walked onstage and started to sing in a smoky, almost raspy voice, he was amazed. From the looks his brothers were giving, he knew they were equally impressed. She was obviously quite talented. When her eyes landed on them, she seemed to relax, as if they were somehow an anchor for her. He wanted to shout out his happiness. They were already starting to form a bond. Then Alyssa had gone up to sing, and Clint had just wanted to hold Bella in his arms. Holding her close, he felt almost consumed with possessiveness. He wanted to claim her in front of everyone so there would be no question as to whom this woman belonged to, the Colton brothers.

Now, as he rubbed her back and saw his brothers closing in to create a protective circle around her, he had the feeling of home. This was how it was going to be from now on. They had found their woman, and now they just needed her to stay with them.

* * * *

Bella calmed down as the brothers surrounded her. She felt safe in Clint's arms, with Clay and Cody rubbing her back and arms. She slowly pulled away and realized how truly tired she was. She yawned and smiled up at the men who surrounded her.

"Will you walk me back to the motel? I think I'm ready for bed now," Bella said to Clint.

Clint, Clay, and Cody all smiled down at her. "Of course, baby, let's get you tucked in," Clay answered.

Bella found Alyssa sitting at the bar. She had been watching them with a gleam of curiosity in her eyes. Bella walked over and hugged her. "Good night, I'm going to go back to the motel. Do you wanna walk with us, or are you staying?"

"I think I'm going to stay for a little bit, maybe have another drink. I'll leave soon," Alyssa told her.

Justin walked over with some water. "Don't worry, I'll make sure she gets home safe," he said as he handed the glass over to a glaring Alyssa. Alyssa wasn't used to men bossing her around or cutting her off when she wanted to drink.

Bella smiled and shook her head. "Okay, I'll see you tomorrow then," she said as she walked toward her men. They were waiting for her at the door. She had to stop thinking that way. They weren't her men.

As Bella walked toward the door, she heard an irate Alyssa say, "Where the fuck is my drink?"

Justin quickly answered, "Ladies shouldn't curse. It doesn't sound attractive."

Alyssa yelled back, "Oh yeah? Well, fuck you!"

Bella turned her head and saw Grant standing behind Alyssa, and Justin smirking at her from behind the bar. Uh-oh, this wasn't going to be good.

Bella turned back to walk toward the bar, when Cody stepped in and took her arm. "Don't worry, beautiful. Justin and Grant won't do anything to Alyssa that she doesn't want." He was smiling down at her.

Bella peeked over her shoulder and saw Alyssa, Justin, and Grant deep in conversation. She realized that her friend was going to be okay and walked with Cody to a waiting Clint and Clay.

# Chapter 5

Cody guided Bella toward his brothers. He hadn't been sure if he was going to be able to talk her into walking away from Alyssa. He knew that Alyssa was safe with Justin and Grant. They had all grown up together, and he could tell that they were both interested in Alyssa. Three single, beautiful women had come into town today, and all three were already spoken for. That's how quickly men in this town needed to move, since the ratio of men to women was so high.

Cody was so grateful that he and his brothers had found Bella. They had been ready to move forward with finding a wife they could all love. Clint was the oldest, at forty, then Clay at thirty-seven, and he was thirty-four. They all grew up in Coltmann County and had returned a few years ago when their parents were ready to retire. Running a ranch was hard work, and his parents were getting on in years and couldn't do the work any longer.

All three of them had gone out on the road, following the bull-riding circuit and looking for adventure. They were ready to settle down now, and holding Bella close, he knew that she was the woman for them. It was a feeling he wasn't familiar with. He felt it in his heart, and it worried him.

He was scared, though, that maybe she wouldn't be able to love them all. She might be leaving soon, how could they convince her to stay? They were all concerned that she would be leaving with her friends as soon as the car was fixed. He was able to talk to Beau and Chase and asked them to delay as much as possible. He knew they were interested in Jessica. They agreed to do their best, but they wouldn't lie. They didn't want to start their already rocky relationship off on a bad note. He could understand that. They just needed to work slowly.

When they were outside of the bar, Cody leaned down and took possession of Bella's lips. He had been waiting all night to kiss her again. While watching Clint dance closely with her, he had been wishing he could cut in and take her into his arms. He was so turned on he could barely get his raging libido under control. He needed to so that he didn't scare her away. He was eating at her mouth and holding her tightly in his arms. Slowly, he eased the kiss into something gentler. He said everything he could with that kiss. *I love you. I need you. Please don't leave me.* When he finally pulled away, Bella was breathing hard, her cheeks flushed and her pupils dilated. Cody leaned down once more and gave her a gentle kiss on her forehead.

* * * *

Bella could barely stand. Cody had given her the most amazing kiss. Her lips were on fire. She focused on getting her breathing under control and then stepped out of his arms. She took Clint and Clay's hands, and they all started walking back to the motel. It was only about a block or two away, so the walk would help her to calm down and focus. She had to remind herself that they had just arrived in town today and that it was a good possibility they were leaving tomorrow. She desperately wanted to spend more time with them, to get to know them. However, time wasn't on her side.

After walking in a comfortable silence, they reached the motel. Bella stopped in front of her door and turned toward the men. She gathered her courage and said, "Would you like to come in? I really don't want this night to end yet."

Clint stepped forward. It was obvious that, with him being the oldest, he was in charge. "Are you sure? We don't want to rush you. There is plenty of time to get to know one another."

"I'm sure. I don't know how much time we have. And if we are leaving tomorrow, I want to be with you, all of you," Bella explained.

Clay stepped forward then, followed quickly by Cody. "If you're sure, baby, then we can take this night slow. Whatever you want, just tell us. We want to make your fantasies come true," he said with a smile.

"My fantasy is to be with the three of you." Bella smiled back at them. She found herself instantly surrounded by warmth once more, and she opened her motel room and walked in.

* * * *

The men surrounded her and gently started to caress and touch her, wanting to get her used to their hands. Clint took her mouth in a passionate kiss as Cody and Clay slowly undressed her. Clay unbuckled her shoes and massaged each foot as he took off her shoes. He paid close attention to the small arches, and when he heard her gentle moan, he knew it was time to move on to the rest of her foot.

Cody pulled off her tank top and started to explore her naked breasts. "Baby, your breasts feel so good, soft here"—he circled her breast with his calloused hands—"and harder here." He tweaked her nipples and then pinched them lightly between his thumbs and forefingers.

Bella arched in between them. They were consuming her. Clint possessed her mouth as Cody played with her breasts, and Clay was running his hand up and down her jeans. Bella arched as Cody continued to examine her breasts, lightly pinching and pulling on her nipples. She started to whimper, needing more. She was half naked, standing in the middle of three gorgeous men. This was the most mind-blowing experience she had ever had, and it was just starting. How was she supposed to keep her sanity?

Bella felt a hand undo her jeans. She heard the zipper being lowered and knew that Clay was obviously running out of patience as well. Clay lowered her jeans slowly and pulled them off. She was now wearing only a pair of white lace panties. She felt vulnerable and at their mercy, and grew hotter.

Clint slowly started kissing down her neck, nibbling on her shoulder as he sank to his knees in front of her. "Look at these beautiful breasts," he said to his brothers. "I could just eat her up." With that, he started licking her nipples, just using his tongue.

Bella leaned into him, hoping that he'd put his whole mouth on her and suck.

Clint laughed a little. "Was there something you wanted, baby?" he asked with a sexy drawl.

Bella looked down at him, on his knees. "I need more," she begged.

Clint continued to torment her breasts as Clay and Cody started running their hands over her body. "Don't worry, baby, we'll give you so much more," Clay told her.

Bella felt a hand—she didn't know whose, and really didn't care—over her mound.

"Your pussy is wet, baby," Clay said, and the tension in his voice was obvious. "You're so hot. Maybe we should take these panties off."

She was soaking wet and feeling completely exposed. She heard a rip and felt her panties being torn off her. The way Clay ripped them off made her even wetter. God, she needed them. She was moaning uncontrollably now. They all stood. Clint picked her up and carried her to the bed.

"Uh-uh," she heard Clint say. "Keep those thighs wide open."

With her thighs open, they all had a clear view of her pussy. Clint's eyes darkened as he reached for her and ran his fingers through her soaked folds. He slowly used one large finger and gently pushed it inside her. Lying naked on the bed, she had all their attention. She felt so sexy, more than any other time in her life. Clay and Cody started to get on the bed next to her, gently caressing her, rubbing and fondling her breasts, arms, and legs.

Bella was shaking with desire, and she wanted them so badly she was willing to do anything and everything. She wanted, no needed, to be fucked by these men. "Please," she whimpered.

"Please what, sweetheart?" Clint asked. He knew what he was doing to her, what they were doing to her, and she needed more. His finger was in her pussy, and he was slowly pumping it in and out. They knew she was aroused, and they continued to tease and torment her.

She started to move on his finger, not caring, just needing more.

"She's so tight and wet, Clay. Why don't come down here and taste our beautiful baby?" Clint said.

She heard Clay moan as he moved in between her splayed legs. He put her feet on his shoulders as he slowly inhaled her pussy. He parted her folds with his thumbs, and Bella started to squirm. He lowered his mouth and started licking slowly, building up a rhythm, exploring her pussy. Clay moaned again, enjoying her taste. He slid his hands under her ass, pulled her closer to his mouth, and devoured her. She was in absolute heaven.

Bella opened her eyes to see Clint and Cody's naked, hard bodies. She hadn't even realized they had undressed. She was disappointed she had missed the show. They were both stroking their cocks, and Bella gasped. Those things were huge. How was she going to be able to fuck them?

Clint must have noticed her look, because he said, "Don't worry, baby, we'll fit." He gave her a little wink.

"Cody, I want you to put something in Bella's mouth," Clint instructed.

Cody had a huge smile as he climbed onto the bed by Bella's face. He was stroking his cock slowly. Some pre-cum was already dripping out. Bella licked her lips, ready to take him.

"Oh yeah, baby, get that sexy mouth ready," Cody told her.

Cody leaned in close, and Bella opened her mouth. His flavor exploded on her tongue. He tasted spicy and delicious. She used both her hands to hold his cock, while she used her tongue and licked up and down his shaft. Then she concentrated on the head, sucking it hard with greedy pulls, just to get his cum to shoot out.

Cody was moaning and shoving his cock into Bella's mouth. "Oh God, baby, that feels fuckin' amazing. I'm not gonna last long. Shit, Clay, make her come, man." Cody was so close. She worked her mouth enthusiastically, knowing she had him on edge. She wanted him to come first, wanted him to lose his control. Just like she was losing hers.

Clay was pulling on her clit and now renewed his efforts to make her come. He shoved a big finger in her pussy, quickly added another, found her G-spot, and rubbed it. She was drenching his fingers, and the walls of her pussy were clamping down. She was close. With his other hand, he slapped her clit. He pumped his finger in a couple more times as Bella's muscles grew tight, her pussy convulsed, and she shrieked around Cody's cock.

Bella renewed her strokes when she felt herself getting closer. She wanted to taste Cody as she came. Her climax stormed through her, just as hot ropes of cum shot of out Cody, and he bellowed in completion. She continued to suck, lick, and kiss his cock until he was totally spent in her mouth. Slowly he withdrew and on shaky legs got off the bed. Bella was breathing hard. That one climax wasn't enough, and her body still needed more.

When she opened her eyes, she was staring at Clint, his cock already sheathed as he stood between her splayed legs.

"You're so beautiful when you come, baby. Are you ready for my cock?" He guided his cock right to the opening of her pussy and slowly pushed in.

He was huge, and even though she was soaking wet, his cock still stretched her.

"Fuck, she's so tight, she's choking my cock," Clint told his brothers.

Bella was squirming now. She needed him to be inside her. She wanted to feel his cock completely in her pussy.

"Hold still, baby. We need to take this slow. I don't want to hurt you," Clint told her.

It was too late. Bella was too far gone. She wrapped her ankles around his back and pulled him quickly toward her until he was fully seated.

Clint tried to calm down his breathing. He was fully seated inside her pussy, and he could feel her muscles squeezing him. "Baby, you feel fantastic." Clint moaned, "So tight." He groaned. He slowly pulled out and then gently pushed back in; starting a slow, gentle pace, but Bella was having none of that.

"Clint, I need you. Please fuck me hard," she begged. She was throwing her hips up to meet his thrusts. That seemed to snap his control, and he started to pound his cock in and out of her pussy.

Bella felt a dip and looked over to see Clay on his knees, stroking his cock. "Open up, baby. I've been dreaming about that mouth."

Bella opened her mouth, and Clay's taste was sweet. She couldn't get enough. She felt amazing and powerful. She used her tongue and did her best to suck him deep into her mouth. Clay started moaning, and she felt his hands smoothing her hair away from her face so that he could watch her.

She arched as Clint fucked her. He was holding her hips in a tight grip, and she couldn't prevent all the mewing noises coming from deep within her throat. Her whole body was on fire, and she was so close to coming again. Never in her life had she been able to come more than once. She squirmed and sucked harder at Clay, wanting him to come after all the pleasure he'd given her. She knew he was close when he gripped her hair tighter in his fist.

"Oh, fuck, I'm gonna come, baby," Clay announced right before he shot his cum into her waiting mouth. He pumped his hips a few more times and then, with a deep sigh, pulled his cock from her mouth.

Clint was getting close. He was amazed he had lasted as long as he had. He moved one hand from her hip to her clit and started rubbing and flicking it. "Baby, it's going to be so amazing when you're riding Clay, and I'm fucking your tight ass and Cody's in your mouth," he whispered to her.

With that thought, she came in a fierce orgasm that completely rocked her world. She was barely aware when Clint yelled, "Fuck, her pussy is milking my cock!" He surged into her twice more and came on a groan.

Bella held Clint close to her until their breathing was once again controlled. He reached up and put his hand on her cheek. She had her eyes closed and a smile on her face. He took her lips in a kiss as both Clay and Cody got onto the bed next to her and started rubbing her body, helping her to relax even more. She kissed him back.

Clint slowly pulled out of her and went to the bathroom to dispose of the condom. When he came back into the room, Bella was asleep in between Cody and Clay. His brothers looked so happy to be holding their woman. He walked over to the bed and looked down at the face of an angel. She had already pushed her way into his heart.

His brothers looked up at him, and Clay whispered, "Are we staying here with her tonight?"

Running a ranch meant that they needed to be up early to do chores. Clint didn't want to leave her here alone. If they did, she might think what they shared was just a quick fuck, instead of the start of something more. "We can't leave her alone. If we do, she might think we only wanted one night," he said. "Cody, why don't you pack her things up? We'll take her with us." That was the only logical thing Clint could think of doing right then. They needed to be at the ranch, and they wanted her to be with them.

Cody got out of bed and got dressed, and then he collected her suitcases and all her belongings. Clint picked Bella up and wrapped the motel blanket around her. Clay wrote a note to her friends. They didn't want them to worry. It was obvious that Bella was exhausted.

She didn't move a muscle as they made their way to the truck and headed toward the ranch. They were all quiet, hoping not to disturb her sleep and hoping that she stayed asleep so that they could get her to the ranch and into their bed. They needed her to be at the ranch. Spending even a minute away from her was no longer acceptable.

# Chapter 6

Bella woke up to the smell of coffee and the sound of birds chirping. She started to stretch, keeping her eyes closed, enjoying the peaceful moment. She felt well rested and smiled, remembering the amazing night last night. Slowly she opened her eyes, wondering if Clint, Clay, and Cody had stayed, or if they had left afterward. As she opened her eyes, and as they adjusted to the light, she realized she wasn't in her motel room.

She jerked herself upright and looked around the huge bedroom. Against one wall were three huge dressers. There were two open doors, one leading into an amazing walk-in closet, and the other she could tell led to a bathroom. She was sitting in the middle of the biggest bed she'd ever seen. It had to be a custom piece. The sheets were a soft blue. The only thought going through her head was *Where am I?* She had woken up naked in a strange place. *This has to be the ranch.* That was the only logical explanation.

Just then, the bedroom door opened, and Clay walked in. "Good morning, beautiful." He walked over to the bed and gently kissed her lips. "Breakfast is ready downstairs. I just came up to get you." Clay pulled the sheets and blankets back. He helped her to climb out of the massive bed. "If I let you stay in that bed too long, I'll climb in there and stay with you." He gave her a smile. "Why don't you go ahead and take a shower? I'll let Clint and Cody know you'll be down soon." He showed her to the massive bathroom.

When Bella walked into the bathroom, she was amazed. Their ranch was absolutely magnificent, and she'd only seen the master bedroom and bathroom. The shower was big enough to fit at least a half-dozen people, and once the water turned on, the showerheads hit her from multiple angles. Bella walked straight into the shower, turned the hot water on, and gave a sign of relief as the hot water sprayed her. She finally felt herself starting to wake up. She scrubbed her body and her hair and quickly got out of the shower. She started to panic when she realized that Jessica and Alyssa had no idea where she was. They were probably freaking out right now.

Bella saw her bags and quickly grabbed a sundress and a pair of flip-flops. She got dressed in a rush and ran downstairs, leaving her bags behind. Clint, Clay, and Cody were all waiting for her around a huge table.

"Good morning, baby, everything okay?" Clint got up and walked over to Bella, concern written on his face.

"I need a ride to the motel. Jessica and Alyssa have no idea where I am. They're going to worry," Bella explained quickly. She started to pace around the huge kitchen.

"Baby, calm down. We left them a note explaining where you were. They aren't expecting you for at least another hour. Why don't you come over and sit down? We made breakfast for you," Clint told her as he pulled her toward the table and sat her down. He leaned over and kissed her, then went to get her a plate of food and some coffee.

Cody leaned toward her and gently kissed her lips. "Baby, we've decided to keep you."

"All right, Cody, calm down. We don't want to scare her away," Clint said as he put the plate in front of her and handed her a huge, hot cup of coffee.

"A girl could get used to this. I feel so spoiled," Bella told them as she started eating her breakfast. *Yummy.* They were great cooks, too. *Jeez, what can't these men do?*

Cody smiled at her and said, "If you stay here, we'll always take care of you."

Bella quickly changed the subject, unsure if life could really happen that way. Could she just move here and be with them? Was there really a happily ever after for her? Everything was happening too fast. Could they really be falling for her the way she was falling for them? She already knew that Coltmann County was a place many people in ménage relationships called home. She wasn't worried about ridicule, but she was a bit concerned with what her family and friends would think if she stayed with them.

"So, do you guys have a lot of work to do today?" Bella asked as she continued to eat.

"We let you sleep in this morning and took care of a large portion of the work already," Clay answered.

"Have you ever been horseback riding?" Clay asked. They wanted her to feel comfortable here and hoped that ranch life would be appealing to her.

"A couple of times, when I was younger, there was a place a few hours away where people could rent horses and go on trail rides. I don't have a lot of experience, but it was fun," Bella answered. She had loved going horseback riding the few times she did. She felt free and a little wild.

"We should plan to take a ride and have a picnic. I'd love to show you our land," Clint told her.

"I'm not sure when we can make a plan to do that. After I meet up with Jessica and Alyssa, we have to figure out what needs to be done to fix the car." Bella smiled back sadly. It felt like this might be good-bye.

"Bella, I know this might seem fast, but even if the car gets fixed today, would you consider staying here with us? I feel like we have something pretty amazing starting here, and to not explore it more seems horrible," Clay interjected. He was feeling as if she was slowly pulling away, and even though they had only met yesterday, they needed time, time to be with her and get to know her better. She also needed to get to know them.

"Um, I'm not sure." Bella looked at each brother and saw only half smiles. Their eyes were sad, though, and she understood that feeling. Could she stay here and let Jessica and Alyssa head on without her? Would her friends be upset if she did tell them she was staying?

* * * *

After Bella ate breakfast, Clint drove her to town. Clay and Cody stayed behind to finish their work. More chores still needed to be done, and since it was only the three of them, their days were filled with work. Clint saw the disappointment on his brothers' faces. They hated to hug Bella good-bye, especially since they didn't know if they were going to see her again. Both Clay and Cody had taken their time kissing her and trying to memorize her taste and smell. None of them reminded her to grab her bags, though. They all wanted an excuse to have her come back to the ranch.

They started the drive down the long dirt road heading for town. Bella stared out the back window, watching both Clay and Cody wave, until she couldn't see them any longer.

"It's so beautiful out here, Clint," Bella said on a quiet sigh. This ranch was perfect, the house, the barn, every part of it. She had wanted to call it home when she woke up. She wasn't upset, because everything just felt so right.

"Promise me that you'll come back here tonight. We need more time, Bella. Even if we arrive in town and your friends are ready to go, I need you to promise me." Clint's voice sounded more like a plea than anything else, and she found herself wanting to please him.

After a few minutes of silence, Bella broke the tension. "Okay, I promise." She looked up at him and smiled. She wasn't ready to leave yet. Now she just had to face Jessica and Alyssa and tell them what was going on. While they were driving away from the ranch and the other brothers, she felt her heart breaking slowly. Right then, she decided that she really did want to find out if this was true love.

* * * *

As they drove into town, the streets were packed full of people. It looked like a huge farmers' market had taken over the main street of the town. Booths were set up, and people were selling different things, from food, to candles, to woodcarvings. It was quite an amazing sight.

"My sister would love this," Bella whispered. Bella and her sister had just started having a relationship. They had different mothers. As kids, they didn't know each other. Now that they were both adults, they tried to meet weekly for coffee or lunch. That was, of course, if their schedules ever matched up.

"Oh yeah? Tell me about your sister." Clint sounded interested. It felt nice to be with a man who really did care about her, who wanted to know more about her life.

Bella shook her head and smiled. "Well, we finally met a couple years ago. We didn't know each other growing up. She's twenty-five. We have different moms. Our dad died. I didn't have a relationship with him. Her name is Hannah. She goes around to different street fairs and farmers' markets. She does face painting, henna tattoos, and she makes jewelry. She's really artistic. I should call her soon. I don't want her to worry." Bella didn't really want to give too much information about her family, but as soon as she started talking to Clint, it was easy to continue. He listened quietly to everything she said, almost mesmerized. It was sweet how interested he really was in learning more about her.

"I'm really close to my mom. She lives down the street from me, and we talk pretty much daily and hang out on the weekends. We've always had a great relationship. My dad, on the other hand, never really was part of the picture. As far as I know, he only had two children. But I'm not positive." Bella was staring out the window at all the people. She didn't want Clint to know of the financial struggles she had growing up. He probably grew up in a loving family with his two brothers. She had always felt alone and disconnected from everyone, except her mom and, of course, her best friends.

"If you decide to stay here with us, you would never have to question our love for you. We would adore you and take care of you forever. Eventually, we'd love to have children as well. I hope you also know that we would do our best to prove to your mom that we can take care of you." Clint looked at her with such love that Bella felt like all the oxygen had been sucked out of the truck's cab. He adjusted his jeans, and she smiled. He was trying to hide his obvious erection. Nothing he did would hide that monster though.

"All of this seems too good to be true. I only just arrived yesterday, and already, you and your brothers are ready for a relationship. It's just too fast. How can you guys even be sure that I'm the one? I'm just the new girl in town. That's all." Bella didn't tell him everything that she was thinking—that eventually, the new-girl image would wear off and they would be stuck with just boring old Bella. She preferred to stay home and read books. Her guilty pleasure was sitting on her patio, reading a book, having a huge coffee, and sneaking a cigarette. Nobody even knew that she enjoyed a smoke every now and then. She wasn't exciting or wild. In fact, being with the three of them was the wildest thing she had ever done in her life. Luckily, that memory would be with her forever.

"Bella, we do know you. You're kind, compassionate, caring, giving, and you have enough love for the three of us. I know this all happened quickly, but you have to know that we have plenty of time. We want you to get used to us and to the idea of the four of us being involved in a loving relationship. You should know that we won't give up on you." His voice became firmer as he spoke.

They drove in silence down the busy street and found a parking spot. Clint quickly got out of the truck and opened the door for Bella. He really wanted to show her that this could work, but he wasn't sure they had enough time. If she decided to leave, they would have to come up with a different plan. Maybe one of them could go to

California and keep wooing her. Clint really didn't think trying to have a long-distance relationship would work out.

Clint took Bella's hand in his as they started walking down Main Street. She was so happy. She smiled, waved, and greeted everyone she passed. She was so polite and stopped at various booths.

"This is so beautiful. Did you make these?" she asked Sam Justice at his booth of woodcarvings.

"Yeah, I've made everything here." He actually blushed at the compliment.

Although most of the men there seemed to be blushing, Bella was walking around complimenting them all. Clint was so proud of her. She wasn't some shy little thing. She was outgoing and kind to everyone.

"Oh, wow, my mother would love this." She picked up a puzzle box that was very intricate in design.

Clint reached into his pocket and grabbed some cash. He pulled out a twenty and handed it to Sam. "Then your mom should have it."

The smile she gifted him with was well worth it. When she grabbed his shirt and pulled him down for a scorching kiss, he would've done anything for her. She was so sincere.

They continued to walk hand in hand down the street. They stopped at various booths along the way to purchase little knickknacks and fresh produce. When they reached the end of the block, they were in front of Austin Brothers' auto shop. From the front window, Bella could see Jessica talking to Beau and Chase. Clint held her hand a little tighter as they headed toward the door. It was obvious that he was nervous when it came to what they were saying.

# Chapter 7

Clint opened the door to Austin Brothers' and allowed Bella to walk in first. The conversation between Beau, Chase, and Jessica came to a stop as they all looked over at the intruders.

"Oh, thank goodness, Bella, I was just asking these two to take me out to the ranch to check on you." Jessica quickly walked over to her and hugged her. It was obvious from Jessica's actions that she had been truly worried.

"I'm sorry to have worried you. I was safe, though. Clint, Clay, and Cody took care of me. How's the car?" That was the main question concerning her. She needed to know if they were able to drive out of town today or not. Then she could deal with the men and make a decision.

"It's horrible, actually. We are officially stranded here." Jessica was upset. She had been crying as well. Her eyes were puffy, and her nose was bright red. It looked as though Beau and Chase were trying to comfort her. Beau was rubbing her back in gentle circles. Chase was holding her arm. It was nice to see Jessica accepting their help.

Clint stepped up. "How bad is it?" He aimed his question at Beau and Chase.

* * * *

Chase, still holding on to Jessica's arm, started to explain what they had found when they had looked at the car this morning. "When we opened the hood, it was clear there was something seriously wrong. Upon closer inspection, the radiator hose had burst. It looks like we have some parts to order."

There was quite a bit that Chase left unsaid, particularly because he didn't want to see Jessica more upset than she already was. This was preventable. The first sign of trouble on the road, and she should've pulled over. A simple fix, that's all it would've taken.

"It looks like we'll be here for a while. We have to order parts and then get everything fixed so that we can make it home." Jessica began to pace, and silent tears were streaming down her cheeks. She put her back to them all, in need of a private moment.

"Angel, why don't we go get something to eat? We can talk about this and figure out the best solution. You aren't alone. You don't need to worry about this right now." Beau's voice was soft as he approached Jessica. He walked up behind her and slowly pulled her back up against his front. While she stared out the window, he slowly rocked her in his arms and let her cry.

Chase walked up and joined them, walking in front of Jessica to surround her with their support. Jessica leaned forward, putting her head on Chase's chest. She wrapped her arms around him and allowed them to hold her. After a few minutes, she was able to calm down and sniffed when she looked up into Chase's eyes.

"That's a good idea. I'm hungry anyway. We should probably find Alyssa. I'm sure after my yelling tantrum that she'll want to know everything is going to be okay."

* * * *

Bella saw the tenderness in the scene that played out in front of her. Jessica was so used to being in charge and handling everything that it must have been hard for her to allow Beau and Chase to comfort her. Bella leaned into Clint. She wanted to help Jessica, but she realized that these men were going to take care of her.

Beau and Chase took Jessica's hands and headed out the door, with Clint and Bella following closely behind. They started walking across the street toward the café and saw Alyssa talking with Justin and Grant. When Alyssa saw them, she said her good-byes and walked toward them. They all walked into the café together and sat in a large booth. After such an emotional morning, everyone was ready for some good food and conversation.

Alyssa, who was obviously curious about where Bella had been, immediately started asking questions. "So, Bella, where were you? The note said you went with Clint, Clay, and Cody to their ranch. I know you left Spread Eagle with them last night, but I had no idea you were heading home with them." She laughed at her own joke and winked knowingly.

Bella squirmed as all eyes turned toward her. "Well, I'm not going to sit here and have girl talk in front of all these men. Jeez, Alyssa, we can talk about this later. I went to the ranch with them last night. It's amazing. I can't wait to go back there tonight." Bella looked sideways at Clint, gauging his reaction to her words. She had just invited herself back to the ranch, taking a big step. A slow smile spread across his lips as her words sank in.

"Are you planning on staying there for the rest of our vacation?" Alyssa wasn't subtle at all. She wanted answers, but she would just have to wait. She was smiling now and leaning partially over the table, whispering, as if no one else could hear her words.

"Yeah, I'm staying at the ranch." Bella wasn't going to beat around the bush, might as well tell everyone that she planned to stay with her men. From the looks she received from her friends, they knew exactly what was happening at the ranch, and they wanted all the juicy details.

"If you ladies don't want to stay at the motel, we do have a guest house of sorts on our property that you could stay in. That way you could save a little money," Clint offered. He might as well do as much as possible to keep Bella's friends in town. The small guesthouse that was on their property sat empty most of the year. It belonged to their parents when they came to visit. Their parents came home during the winter months, and they liked their privacy.

Bella smiled appreciatively. "That's perfect. Thank you, honey." She received a few curious looks from her friends. She leaned over and kissed him. "What do you think? Save money and have some extra time to think what we're gonna do?"

Alyssa and Jessica glanced at each other quickly, and then Jessica answered for them both, "That would be great, Clint, thank you."

Everyone ordered their food and ate in a comfortable silence, mostly because they were hungry. Beau and Chase watched Jessica while they ate, making sure she was feeling better. Clint had his hand on Bella's thigh and leaned over every few minutes to kiss her cheek or put her hair behind her ear. He looked so happy that she had agreed to come back to the ranch. She couldn't wait to see Clay's and Cody's response.

* * * *

After they all ate lunch, Clint drove the women to the motel to pick up their luggage. Bella was thrilled that Jessica and Alyssa would be able to see the ranch. Since finding out that they were stuck in Coltmann County, Bella used it as an excuse to spend more time with Clint, Clay, and Cody. Everything seemed to be working out, and with a little coaxing, she hoped to convince her friends to stay for the rest of the summer. There was no need for Bella to rush back. Alyssa had already finished the semester. She was in limbo until she decided what her next move was. Jessica needed Internet access. She would need to do work, even if remotely. She could get it done. Maybe if Jessica did some work, she could focus on that and not on her car.

Alyssa and Jessica were packing up their belongings and loading them into the truck, when Bella turned to Clint. "Is there any Internet at the guesthouse? I'm just thinking that if Jess can focus on something else for a little while, she might start to feel better."

"That won't be a problem, baby. There is Internet, don't worry. When we take them to the guesthouse, we'll let them get comfortable, and I'll let Jessica know the Internet passwords." Chase pulled her close and kissed her lips, just a soft brush that had her heart pounding harder in her chest.

* * * *

They pulled up to the guesthouse. It was a few miles away from the main house. The house was a cute, rustic-looking place, with all the amenities. A full wraparound patio gave it a welcoming feel. Three wooden rocking chairs sat on the patio outside a pair of double doors that led inside the house. It was a creamy brown color with green trim and matching shutters.

"This place is great. I can see why your parents must love it here. It feels relaxing, and it's so quiet," Jessica said as she gathered her luggage. She took a deep breath, and the tension in her shoulders slowly dropped.

"I did want to tell you that this place has wireless Internet, cable, with all the movie channels you could possibly want, and the pantry is stocked. The fridge does have a few things, but anything else you might need we can get at the store in town. I'll bring one the of the work trucks over for you both to use if you need to drive into town at all." Clint walked into the house, carrying their luggage and showing them around. The house was kept clean for when their parents arrived. "I'll leave you both to unpack and get settled. If you need anything, my cell number and the house number are next to the phone. Please make yourselves at home." Clint walked out of the house and closed the door.

Jessica took her time, walking around, looking at all the family pictures. She found a room and started to unpack her clothes. She needed a vacation and promised herself that, regardless of what happened, she would relax and try to enjoy the peaceful environment.

If she did get bored, she could always pull her laptop out and do some work. There was always work to be done. She took a moment to sit on the bed and think. Everything would be fine, the car would get fixed, and they would go home. In the meantime, she would just try to go with the flow.

# Chapter 8

Clint opened the passenger side door and helped Bella get into the truck. He reached over to help her buckle the seat belt and rubbed his forearm against her breast. Her nipples pebbled as he heard her quick intake of breath. She was as horny as he was. She was just better at disguising it. The whole morning, he'd kept adjusting himself so that he wouldn't embarrass himself with a monster erection, walking around town and having lunch with Bella and her friends. Clint reached up and caressed her soft cheek, then leaned in and kissed her lips.

"I want to get you to the ranch, baby, so we can all love you together." Clint slowly pulled back from the kiss and closed the door. He walked quickly over to his side and jumped in. Clint's thoughts were consumed with images of Bella as he started driving toward the main house. Luckily, the drive wouldn't take too long. He was restless. His balls felt heavy and ached with the pressure of denied release. Judging by Bella's intense stare out the window, she was probably feeling the same. Clint was excited that Bella wasn't shy. She enjoyed sex just as much as they did. She didn't hold her passion back from them, and he really wanted to experience more with her.

Bella started to scoot closer to him on the bench seat while he was lost in thought. She placed her hand on his thigh and started rubbing it in circles, moving closer to his cock. Then she leaned over and licked his neck. Bella was obviously ready for more. His last coherent thought was that he just needed to get home as soon as possible. They were only about a mile away, so they would be there in a matter of seconds.

As Clint sped down the dirt road, he saw Clay and Cody come out of the barn, his erratic driving having alerted them of trouble. He slammed on the brakes, shoved the gear into park, and took the keys from the ignition. He jumped out of the truck, walking quickly to the passenger side. He pulled Bella out and threw her over his shoulder. Forget finesse. He needed to shove his cock into her pussy now. He wasn't going to last long, but he planned to make it up to her during the next round.

Clay and Cody were staring at him with shock and excitement as Clint yelled out, "Hurry up! We've got a woman to please. Master bedroom, now."

He didn't have to say any more than that. His brothers took off for the house, opened the doors for him, and stripped on the way to the bedroom. It seemed that they all were in desperate need of some loving. Clint walked straight into the bedroom and dropped Bella on the bed. He immediately started taking off his clothes. He needed to get his cock out of the confines of his jeans. They all stood naked before her and gave her a minute to look her fill before they all got onto the bed and started removing the barriers between them and her soft, naked flesh.

Clint climbed up Bella's body, kissing her stomach, the underside of her breasts, her neck, and when he got to her mouth, he kissed her deeply, enjoying her tongue against his. He ate at her mouth, moving to the side of her body to allow Cody access to her pussy. He heard her gasp and moan and assumed that Cody had started licking her.

Clint pulled away from her mouth and moved his big body down so that he could suck on her perfect nipples. He needed another taste. They had taunted him all day under her sundress. Clint made eye contact with Clay as he moved from Bella's mouth, and gave a knowing smile. Clay was waiting for his turn at her mouth. He had his hand on his cock and was slowly pumping it up and down.

Clint rolled his tongue over one nipple and started to suck it. He used his hand on the other nipple, rolling it and pinching it. Bella seemed to like her pleasure with a little pain. She was writhing on the bed, pushing her pussy firmly onto Cody's mouth while lifting her breasts further into his mouth.

Clay got onto the bed and positioned himself right in front of Bella's face. Like a starving woman, Bella went after Clay's cock, sucking him deep. A thought flashed through Clint's mind that they had found a perfect woman in Bella. She didn't play games with them, needing to be led into every encounter. She didn't hide the fact she loved sex or the fact she obviously loved cock. She was embracing what they offered wholeheartedly.

Clint watched Cody and Clay. He knew they were as worked up as he was. They were trying to take things at a pace that was comfortable for Bella, not wanting her to feel scared. She was a pleasant surprise to them all. She dove right into the excitement, giving and receiving with equal enthusiasm. They wanted her to come before they moved forward, and from what he could see, Cody was doing everything is his power to have her come.

* * * *

Cody was licking Bella up and down from her beautiful little rosebud to her gorgeous, delicious pussy. He wanted to taste her. He wanted her cum all over his face. With that thought, he brought his fingers into play. He slowly twirled his fingers around her clit and gently pushed them into her pussy. He soaked them with her juices and then started pumping them into her. He held on to her hip tightly with his other hand, and she bucked and squirmed. He looked and made eye contact with Clint, sending him a silent message.

Clint gave him a slight nod, and he started whispering to Bella, "Cody's enjoying the taste of you, baby. I can't wait to get my mouth on that pussy. Do you like that, baby? Do you like having your pussy licked?"

* * * *

Bella was in heaven. All three of her men were as desperate as she was. Cody had his face buried in her pussy, and Clint was sucking her nipples, pinching and playing with her. When Clay climbed onto the bed, she couldn't contain herself. She went after his cock like a starving woman. They were giving her so much pleasure, and in turn, she wanted to pleasure them. She just tried to focus on the feel of them. "Oh God! It's never been this good!" She listened to Clint's erotic words while Cody was licking her and she was sucking on Clay's cock. This was her undoing. Bella grabbed Clay's cock and sucked harder while Cody clamped down on her clit. Almost at the same time, Clay shouted his release. Bella let go of his cock. "Ohhh! Ahhh!" The most amazing feeling washed over her, and she grabbed for her men desperately.

*Oh, wow...*Her mind went blank as the world spun all around her. Pleasure pulsed through her. The intensity scared her a little bit. As she lay there, trying to get her heartbeat under control, she felt the bed dip and heard the bathroom water turn on. Clay must have gone into the bathroom.

Clint watched from his position next to Bella as Cody stood up and slid a condom onto his cock. He looked ready to ram it into her, but instead he caressed her stomach and hips. The touch was tender.

Cody leaned down and took possession of her lips before he said, "Bella, Clint's going to lie down in the middle of the bed. I want you to climb on top of him and put that beautiful pussy on his cock."

Clint's cock jerked when he heard his brother's words. It seemed that it was time to move forward. Cody was taking control.

"After your pussy is packed full of his cock, I'm going to get your ass nice and ready. Do you know what's going to happen next? Clint's gonna fuck your pussy while I fuck your ass." Clay could tell that his words were making Bella excited. Her eyes were still glossy, and there was a spark of fire.

Bella slowly turned over and crawled toward Clint, who was lying on the middle of the bed. He had a condom lying on the bed next to him. She moved up his body, kissing his chest, licking his nipples, on the way up to his full lips. She kissed him, nibbling on his full lower lip for a minute, before grabbing the condom. She sat up, straddling his chest, and opened the condom, and slid it down his massive erection. He groaned but kept his eyes open to look at her while she worked him up and down. To his utter amazement, she then lowered herself onto his shaft. Her eyes fluttered closed, and she moaned in enjoyment at the feel of him in her. After she rose up and fell down on his cock, Cody's hands gripped her hips and stopped her movements.

"Slow down, baby. Lean forward and hold on to Clint. I'm going to start stretching your ass now." Cody kissed her neck and shoulder. Clay handed him the tube of lubricant. "Clay, why don't you rub her back? Then you can hold her ass cheeks apart while I work my fingers in and out of her." They were all involved now, touching, rubbing, kissing, and caressing.

* * * *

Cody spread a liberal amount of lubricant on his finger and started by making small circles around her rosebud. "Take a deep breath, baby, and relax your muscles. This may feel a bit foreign at first, but I'll take good care of you. Okay now, love, deep breath, hold it, and push out. Good job. My finger is sliding in you. Tell me what you're feeling?" Cody was trying to take things slow, but he needed them to all be together.

"Oh, it hurts and burns…" She was panting.

"You're doing perfect, sweetie. I'm going to add another finger now. Keep breathing and push out."

Clint and Clay were both rubbing her body with their strong hands, massaging her back and buttocks. Cody added another finger and more lube, pumping his fingers in and out of her gently. She was almost ready for him. He could tell that both Bella and Clint were ready for more. Their breathing had increased.

Cody added more lubricant on his sheathed cock and positioned himself at her rosebud. "Okay, baby, deep breath, I'm going to push my cock in you now. No, don't tense up. Relax." He rubbed her hip with one hand while he used his other to guide his cock into her waiting hole.

Clint sank his fingers into her hair. "You're perfect, baby. Look at me, and focus on me. Cody will be gentle. Being inside you feels better than anything I've ever felt. Cody and Clay want to feel you, too, baby. We'll take care of you." Clint was holding her attention and reassuring her, which helped to relax her while Cody moved forward.

"I'm in." Cody was panting, trying to hold on to his control. He really wanted to start pounding, but she needed time to adjust. "Okay, Bella, Clint and I are gonna do all the work, baby. I just want you to feel and focus on keeping these muscles relaxed."

He pulled out slowly and then pushed back in. Before long, Cody and Clint set up a slow rhythm, pushing in and pulling out of her body. When she cried out at a deeper trust, Clay was there, murmuring tenderly to her. Clay caressed her thighs and arms, praising her as she took Cody and Clint's thick lengths into her body.

Cody held on to her tightly, putting his chest against her back so that he could whisper to her, "You're so beautiful, baby. Your skin is flushed and pink. I won't ever get enough of you." He continued his slow strokes, working his cock deeper into her body.

"It's like fucking a soft glove. God, baby, your pussy is clamping down on me." Clint's breathing was becoming harsher. Perspiration was gathering on his forehead. He needed to move faster. At a nod to Cody, they started a quicker pace, with deeper thrusts.

* * * *

Bella was fisting Clint's chest. He had such soft skin, and with his muscles flexing, it excited her more. "It's too much. I'm close, oh God!" Cries and moans were coming out of her. She hadn't realized that it was her own voice until she screamed. Feeling Clint and Cody moving inside her made her feel naughty, but it also made her feel complete in a way she had never felt before. Nothing had ever felt this good. She didn't want this feeling to end, being held tight in between them, being controlled and loved by them all. With one hand, Bella reached out and started rubbing Clay. She wanted him to get closer to her. She reached for his cock but couldn't reach. When he noticed she wanted him closer, he moved so he could be.

She wanted them to all share in this moment. She pumped her hand on his cock. "Clay, I need your cock in my mouth." She was panting and close to coming, but she really needed Clay to be a part of this moment. She wanted all her men together.

"Nice and easy, baby." Clay held her hair in his fist. He watched her sucking his cock. Clint and Cody were moving faster, which had her groaning in her throat. Clay started fucking her mouth with smooth, short strokes.

Having all three of them, she felt consumed by lust and warmth. Bella couldn't imagine being more aroused than she felt at this moment. Her bottom burned. This foreign sensation of having her ass fucked was amazing.

"She feels fucking amazing. I'm not gonna last," Clay announced.

She didn't think it would have been possible to take something so deeply into her ass. She screamed in her throat when he plunged even deeper and gripped her hips tightly, forcing himself to the hilt inside her as he shot his release. It wasn't enough. She needed more. *Oh God.* She was frantic now, sucking hard on Clay's cock.

"Damn it, she's close, Clint. Rub her clit. Let's send her over," Cody said.

Clint reached down in between their bodies and touched her clit. That was all she needed.

Bella screamed out her release. In all her life, she never remembered ever coming this hard. Clint grabbed her hips and pumped in two more times before he bellowed out his release. She collapsed against Clint's chest. Holding on to him tightly, she squeezed her eyes closed. Everything was spinning. She hadn't realized she was crying until Clint started rubbing her back. He was holding her tightly against his chest. Other hands joined his, touching her and massaging her. Her men surrounded her, and she felt so loved. She swallowed the huge knot in her throat. The tears wouldn't stop, and she quietly sobbed against Clint.

"Baby, are you okay? We didn't hurt you, did we?" Cody's concerned voice was able to reach her.

"No," Bella sniffed. "I don't know why I'm crying. I'm happy. I'm sad. I don't know where this is going. I don't know if this will even work." She took a deep breath. She didn't want to talk about this right now. They had just had an amazing experience, and here she was being an emotional girl. Damn it, this was probably going to push them away. What man wanted a crying girl to deal with? She buried her face further into Clint. God, she was so embarrassed.

"Clay, why don't you go start a bath for our girl? Add some bath salts so that she can relax. I'll carry her in. We don't want her to be sore." Clint pushed her hair out of her face and lifted her up so that she was facing him. "Bella, don't hide yourself from us. We want to be here for you through the good times and the not-so-good ones. This thing we have, it's special, and you mean a lot to all of us."

Clint stood up slowly, holding Bella close to his chest and scooted out of bed. Cody was standing at the edge of the bed and helped Clint stand.

Clay was leaning against the bathroom door, watching the scene unfold. "The bath is ready," he told them.

Clint walked directly to the bathroom, with Bella in his arms, and slowly lowered himself into the warm tub. Bella moaned as the water touched her skin. It felt good. She stayed in Clint's arms while she heard a small splash and felt the water rise.

"Mmmmm, this was a great idea, Clint," Cody said, and he moved over to make room for Clay. They both reached for her, and Clint turned Bella around so her back was to his front. Clay and Cody both reached for a foot and started to massage.

Clint massaged her shoulders. He kissed her neck and whispered, "Just relax, baby, and let us take care of you."

Bella leaned back and enjoyed the attention her men gave her. She closed her eyes and moaned loudly. "That feels so good. Oh God, don't stop. I had no idea that my muscles were so tight." Bella turned to mush and completely leaned into Clint. "Hmmm, a girl could get used to this."

Clint laughed silently. Bella felt his laugh through her body. She peeked out from under her eyelashes. Cody and Clay were both smiling.

"Well, baby, don't you worry. We'll take good care of you." Clay used his sexy Texas drawl as he pressed his fingers expertly into Bella's foot.

Bella's smile broadened. Yep, a girl could sure get used to this.

"Are you feeling better, baby?" Cody asked. "You never answered Clint." It was obvious from his tone that he was concerned. Did he feel that he had hurt her? Or that he'd gotten too rambunctious while they were fucking?

Bella pulled her feet out of their hands and climbed toward Cody. She wanted to reassure him. She moved through the huge Jacuzzi tub and climbed into his lap. "I'm fine, Cody. I promise you didn't hurt me. I'm not sure why I cried, except that it was an emotional moment." She sighed deeply. "There was just so much going on. With all of you touching me, I felt loved." Bella leaned into him, wrapping her arms around his neck, and kissed his cheek. She cuddled close in his lap, hoping that he would believe her. Cody rubbed her back and held on to her tight, comforting her.

"I'm glad you're okay, baby." Cody held her. He let out a deep breath. “We would never want to hurt you. We’ll work everything out. Let us take care of you.”

Clint and Clay were ready to wash her. They had the washcloth already soaped up and were reaching toward her when Cody turned her around. Clint washed her legs, moving up toward her pussy, while Clay lathered her arms and moved toward her breasts.

“We’re crazy about you. I hope you know that we’re not willing to let you go. We are going to love you, spoil you, and treat you so good that you’ll never want to leave,” Cody whispered in her ear.

Bella smiled, knowing that there was nowhere she wanted to be but with them.

Clint and Clay rinsed her and washed the rest of her. Bella slowly closed her eyes.

“Okay, baby, time to get out.” Clay got out first, dried off quickly, and reached to take Bella from Cody. He helped her out of the tub, wrapped a towel around her, and started drying her off as Clint and Cody got out and dried themselves off.

When Clint was finished drying off, he picked up Bella and carried her to the bed. Cody walked to the bed with some lotion he’d found in her bag. Bella fell asleep on the huge bed, with Clint, Clay, and Cody rubbing her body with lotion. Her last thought before she fell into dreamland was *I love you guys.*

* * * *

Clint, Clay, and Cody all looked at Bella. Her whispered words stopped them in the middle of rubbing lotion on her body. She was asleep, breathing evenly. They were silent for a moment, looking at this woman they already loved. They looked at each other, shock apparent on their faces, and then they smiled. Clint looked at his brothers, feeling complete satisfaction.

“Her subconscious is ready to admit to her feelings. We just need her to realize that she loves us,” he told his brothers.

"I love her. Do you think she might stay?" Clay asked his brothers.

"I don't know. All we can do is show her how much we love her. It will work out. She loves us just as much as we love her," Cody told them.

Clint pulled Bella's back against his front. She squirmed a little bit, getting closer to him. He took a deep, relaxing breath. He put his right arm under her pillow and his left arm around her stomach, and he held her close to his body.

He watched both his brothers find a spot on the bed. Clay got onto the other side and put his head against her chest and his right hand on her hip. He kissed her head and fell asleep. Cody watched them, and then he finally moved, getting on the bed with them. He moved his body so that he was still touching her. This whole relationship was new to them, and it would take some time to get used to it, but Clint knew that they all would end up happy.

# Chapter 9

Bella was having the most erotic dream. Multiple sets of hands and mouths were touching her. Openmouthed kisses all over her body, everything felt so real. She woke up on a moan. Large, strong hands were rubbing her. Bella slowly opened her eyes to see Clay smiling at her. He slowly kissed her, moving his way down her body.

"Good morning, baby. I didn't want to wake you, but I couldn't stop myself from touching you. I have a raging hard-on, and I'm waking you up the best way I know how." He didn't stop his journey down her body, only stopped when he was staring at her naked pussy. Her body, smooth, soft, and curvaceous, called to him.

Clay leaned down and moaned as he took his first taste of her pussy. Immediately, Bella jerked, almost dislodging his face. Clay gave a silent laugh as he pulled her closer to his mouth and held her securely.

"Oh no you don't, baby. Keep that pussy against my mouth," he demanded in a rough voice.

Cody leaned over and started kissing her mouth in long, drugging kisses, playing with her lips and gently coaxing them to open. He slid his tongue into her mouth. She loved feeling his tongue against hers. Eventually they set up a rhythm while Clay licked her pussy.

They were both driving her crazy, taking her higher in her arousal. Briefly, she wondered where Clint was but quickly decided to focus on Clay and Cody. Clay was playing with her pussy, licking and sucking on her clit. He soon added his fingers to the mix and played with her pussy and her ass. He slowly pushed two fingers into her pussy, pushing them in and out gently as he sucked her clit. With his other hand, he used just the tip of his finger on her ass, rimming her, getting her ready for penetration. Cody moved his lips, slowly kissing and biting down her neck, working his way to her breasts. He circled one nipple with his tongue, sucking it into his mouth. He bit down, creating a great mixture of pleasure and pain.

"Oh, I'm getting close. Oh God!" Bella was writhing on the bed. She was shaking, so close to the edge. She needed more. She needed something more so that she could fall over into a massive orgasm. She felt it looming, just out of reach. It was becoming aggravating, and she moaned and pushed at them, begging them to give her what she needed.

"Oh, poor baby, you need more, don't you?" Cody pulled back and gave a nod to Clay.

They always did that, seemed to be able to communicate without words. It must be amazing to have the close relationship they did. Clay pulled away.

"No, damn it, don't stop. Fuck, I was so close." Bella started to raise her voice. They knew she was close, so why did they stop?

"Hands and knees, baby, we're gonna help you come," Clay told her, and he helped her move.

This position was her favorite. Their cocks reached farther, and it made her come so hard. Bella moved to her hands and knees, looking over her shoulder at Clay. He slid a condom on his hard cock and applied extra lube. They were always so gentle, making sure that she would be okay.

Clay held her hip with one hand. With the other, he rubbed her ass cheek. "I'm gonna fuck this pussy nice and deep, baby."

She was so excited. She could feel her juices dripping down her thigh. She turned back to face Cody, who was now leaning against the headboard, stroking his cock. Some pre-cum was leaking out the top, and Bella licked her lips.

"Get those lips nice and wet for my cock, baby. Crawl over here and lick the head."

Bella crawled over to Cody and grabbed his cock with both hands. She leaned down and licked the head, pulling the pre-come into her mouth. She moaned when his flavor hit her tongue. He tasted spicy, sweet, and a little salty. She wanted more. She lowered her head to take more into her mouth just as Clay pushed into her pussy.

"Mmmmm," she moaned deep in her throat.

Clay mimicked her pace. The faster she sucked Cody's cock, the faster he would fuck her. She made it a game, teasing Cody and herself in the process.

"No more teasing. I want you to suck Cody nice and deep, baby." Clay held her hips tight and shoved his cock into her repeatedly.

"Fuck, I'm getting close. Keep sucking, baby. Yeah, just like that. Swallow around my cock. Take it as deep as you can."

* * * *

Cody was getting close. The thought of her swallowing his cum took him closer to the edge. He grabbed her head and helped her take him deeper. Holding her hair tightly in his fist, he moved it to the side so he could watch her.

"Oh, baby, I'm gonna come. Swallow it all, baby." Cody shoved his cock into her mouth once more and started to come. Hot jets splashed in her mouth, and she swallowed every bit down. Cody yelled as he came, twitching slightly as he slowed his breathing. He rubbed her head and caressed her cheek.

"Cody, start rubbing her clit. I'm close, and I want her to go over first." Clay was holding Bella's hips tight as he powered in and out of her. He leaned over Bella, gathered some of her juices on his finger, and then started to make slow circles around her rosebud. He pushed an index finger into her ass slowly, making sure she was relaxed. He pushed his finger all the way in, letting her ass adjust, then started pumping it in the same rhythm as his cock. When he was able to, he added another finger.

Bella was losing her mind. "Oh God! I'm gonna come. Fuck me harder, Clay," she demanded. Clay was fucking her so deep, and when he added a finger to her ass, she felt consumed with pleasure. He kept at it, fucking her pussy and her ass. She was shaking and moaning, begging for more. She felt fingers playing with her clit, and just that quick, Bella went over the edge.

"Oh fuck! Fuck! I'm coming! Don't stop, Clay." Bella closed her eyes tight, and the world began to spin. Never in her life had sex been this amazing. She collapsed on the bed right after she heard Clay.

"She's squeezing the life out of me…oh fuck." Then he came. She felt his cock jerk and pulse inside of her.

Clay fell on top of Bella as she went down on the bed. He kissed her shoulder and held her in his arms. They stayed like that until their heartbeats slowed down. When Clay felt like he could stand without falling, he slowly pulled his cock out of Bella and stumbled to the bathroom.

"Well, I guess Bella's awake." Clint was standing against the bedroom door, smiling. "I went downstairs to feed the animals and start the coffee. Guess what I heard when I was in the kitchen? Luckily, I made it upstairs in time to watch you come, baby. I love watching you yell out in abandon, not caring who hears." Her skin turned pink and flushed under his observation.

Bella lifted her head and turned to see Clint smiling down at her. "Time to get cleaned up, baby. We're gonna meet Alyssa and Jessica for breakfast at the café."

Bella smiled and started to sit up. Clint helped her get her bearings before getting out of bed. He put his arms around her, pulling her naked body into his. He kissed her with such passion it brought tears to her eyes. When was she leaving? Could she leave these men behind? Every moment spent with them made her fall more for them. She was going to lose her heart. Before she made herself completely depressed, Bella decided to think positively. She might as well have a good vacation.

Cody walked over, pulled her from Clint, and kissed her, walking her to the bathroom. "Do you need any help taking a shower?"

Bella started laughing. "Yeah right, if any of you step into that shower with me, we'll be here all day." She walked in and shut the door behind her. "I'll be ready in twenty minutes."

Needing a little space and some alone time, she started the water and got in, letting the hot water hit her.

* * * *

When they got to the diner, Jessica and Alyssa were talking to Beau and Chase. They sat around a huge table, toward the back of the café. Bella walked toward the table, Clint, Clay, and Cody close behind her. There weren't any secrets in this town, especially when one woman was with three men. Everyone seemed to know what was going on, and when Bella looked down, Clint knew she was embarrassed. He grabbed her hand before she reached the table, and stopped her.

"What's wrong, baby?" He was concerned. They were walking toward her friends when Bella put her head down and looked shamed. Was she embarrassed to be with them? He started to feel a little insecure, which actually made him angry. They were trying to start a relationship. She couldn't be ashamed and have a relationship with them.

"Everyone is staring at me. It's like they know that we were all together," she whispered. "What if they think I'm some sort of slut?"

"Baby…" Clint pulled her in for a hug so he could whisper in her ear. He knew she didn't understand their town, so he'd better explain. "This town is full of couples in ménage relationships. If people are looking at you and smiling, it's because they are happy that we finally found a woman we all can love and who can love us in return. Nobody here is judging you. You have to remember that we grew up here. We've been waiting for you. The people in this town care about us." He kissed the top of her head, put her hand in his, and pulled her along behind him. Clint felt better knowing Bella's concerns. She would understand more when she met their mom and dads.

Clint had talked to them this morning, knowing that if he didn't say something quick, someone in town would. In a place like Coltmann County, it was better to tell people what was going on before anyone else did. With their parents, someone would have called them sooner rather than later. He didn't want his parents showing up on their doorstep to check Bella out. They still needed a little more time to get her used to the idea of being with them.

Clint wanted to help Bella and ease her fears, so he decided to make a few stops at different tables to introduce her to some of their friends who were in ménage relationships. He also wanted to confirm what he had told her about the people in town that they were looking at them with joy and envy, not in judgment.

Clint walked Bella over to meet some of his best friends he had known since childhood. "Good morning, Shane, Maddox, and beautiful Gina. I want you to meet Bella." He pulled Bella up beside him. "Bella, these two guys went to school with us, and this beautiful lady is their wife, Gina." Clint looked at her face while he made the introductions, waiting for a gasp or any other kind of negative reaction. He hadn't meant to call his friends out, but he needed Bella to know that the people weren't going to judge them.

Bella put her hand out. "Hello, it's nice to meet you all." She smiled at them. Shane, Maddox, and Gina all looked happy and eager to meet her.

"Hi, it's nice to meet you. When you walked in with these guys, we weren't sure we would get an introduction," Gina said with a knowing smile. She sat in a booth with a man on each side. Both Shane and Maddox had a hand on her thigh while they were eating. It looked like they wanted to be even closer but kept a small space because they were in public.

"Bella's friends are waiting for us at the table over there. Did you get a chance to meet them yet? We're hoping to convince them to stay." Clay stepped up, grabbing Bella's other hand. They were making it known that she was taken.

"Yeah, Beau and Chase introduced them on the way in. They said almost the exact same thing you did," Maddox responded with a laugh in his voice.

"It's good to meet you, Bella. We'll all have to get together soon for a barbecue. It's nice during the evening. That way we can sit outside under that huge tree in the yard," Gina suggested.

"That's a great idea, darlin'. We'll plan something for tomorrow evening," Cody said.

"Are you all free tomorrow around six? Bring a side dish. We'll grill up some steaks and burgers," Clint added. This was a perfect idea, everyone out at the ranch, having some fun. Bella would fit right in and realize that she should stay.

"Sounds good. We can bring some of my famous German potato salad. Should we pass the word along?" Gina asked.

"That would be great. Thanks." Clint tipped his head and smiled at his friends. He walked toward the back table where Beau, Chase, and Bella's friends were sitting. He knew the barbecue would bring out everyone, and they would welcome Bella to Coltmann County.

* * * *

"Good news," Jessica sang as Bella and her men sat down around the large round table in the back of the café. "The parts are ordered and should be here Monday. We should be back on the road next week. We can either head home or continue our journey." Jessica had a huge smile on her face, looking back and forth from Bella to Alyssa. She wasn't getting the answer she was looking for, so she continued talking. "What? Aren't you both excited? I thought you would both be happy."

"Th–that's great news, Jess." Bella was a little shocked. She wasn't expecting the car to be fixed so soon. She was feeling a little scared about the future, if she was leaving with her friends or staying with the Colton brothers. It was obvious that the men at the table were less than satisfied with the news. She decided to change the subject, in hopes the mood would change. "How's working remotely?" Bella asked Jessica, hoping she would just answer the question and stop talking about the car or them leaving.

"Great, actually. I've been checking the online orders and then sending the information to Diana. She's been shipping everything. Being an online store, everything is working out great. I can work from anywhere." Jessica was all smiles today. It was nice seeing her in a good mood for a change and not stressed out over work. She always carried everything on her shoulders. "You were right. I'm so glad I came on this trip."

"I'm glad everything is working out. I thought that it might be a good idea to have a girls' day this afternoon. Tomorrow Clint, Clay, and Cody are having a barbecue at the ranch." Bella wanted to have some girl talk away from all the men, and having a day to themselves seemed like the best way to be able to talk.

"I love that idea. I can make my famous dip." Alyssa smiled.

"Where should we go?" Jessica asked.

"There is a small spa here in town. I thought we could pamper ourselves a little and have some girl talk." Bella smiled, remembering all the times they had gotten together for their monthly spa day.

"That's a great idea. While you ladies do that, we can go shopping for supplies for tomorrow. Take the truck. If you need anything, just give me a call," Clint encouraged.

"Okay. We'll head out after breakfast. I'll meet you guys at the ranch when we're done." Bella smiled at her men. She didn't want to miss spending a day with them, but she really needed some girl time, and talking in front of them wasn't a good idea.

* * * *

Bella walked out of the café, kissed her men good-bye, and headed toward the spa with Jessica and Alyssa.

During breakfast, she thought about leaving Coltmann County and the Colton brothers. Her heart felt heavy. She didn't want to leave. Reality and fantasy were battling it out. Reality was she needed to have a job. There really weren't many options in town. Reality number two, her mom lived just down the street from her apartment in San Diego. Moving might be hard on her, and the last thing she wanted to do was hurt her mom. The fantasy, though, was perfection, living with her men, being loved by them, not having to ever worry about being alone again. Could reality and fantasy blend? Could her life really end happily ever after?

She was quietly thinking when Alyssa broke in. "Bella? Hello, are you listening?"

Bella jolted out of her mind and away from those thoughts. "Yeah. I'm sorry, just thinking." She took a deep breath and let it out slowly. This was girl time, so it was time to share. "I'm thinking about the future, if I have one here. I'm just not sure if I'm ready to leave yet." Bella sighed and waited for a reaction.

Alyssa was the first to comment. "I know. I could tell when you met them that you were crazy about them. Do you think it could work?"

Alyssa was looking at her with a mixture of envy and sadness. Bella couldn't figure out the envy, unless Alyssa wanted a relationship. The sadness was easy. Their life was in California. If Bella stayed, they'd be separated.

"I don't know. If I leave, I'll never know. I guess the question should be is it worth staying to see if it does work out?" Bella didn't think she would be able to just pack up her things and say good-bye to them. Their lives were here. It would be selfish to ask them to leave their home, friends, and family. They were established, had a business. She was unemployed and rented an apartment. It just didn't make any sense. The more she thought about it, the more willing she was to stay. She just needed someone else to say she wasn't being crazy.

"That's crazy. You can't move and change your life. What about a job?" Jessica was upset. The happy, smiling friend at lunch was gone. In her place was an in-charge, bossy Jessica.

"I've been thinking about that, and I have a plan of sorts, but I need both of you." Bella smiled and decided not to say any more until she was enjoying a spa pedicure and a back massage. She kept walking to the spa, knowing that they were following behind her. Nobody spoke again, all of them immersed in thought.

# Chapter 10

They walked into the spa. It was small but quite comfortable. The walls were a pale green color. Soft music whispered throughout the building. The spa smelled so amazing, like eucalyptus, lavender, and jasmine. It wasn't overwhelming, just light scents that lingered in the air. The lights were low, and there was a waterfall, adding to the overall atmosphere.

Bella was awestruck. The outside of the building was nice, but it would have gone unnoticed. The inside was decadent and beautiful. Taking a deep breath, Bella let it out slowly, letting her stress and worries go away. She felt a sense of peace wash over her. This place was definitely amazing. She smiled and looked over at her friends, knowing they were just as impressed.

"Good afternoon," a petite woman said. "I'm Ivy Weston. This is my place. Welcome to The Cloud Lounge."

"Hi, this place is wonderful. I'm Bella, and these are my friends Jessica and Alyssa. It's nice to meet you." Bella walked over to Ivy and shook her hand. They were about the same height, but Ivy was thinner. She was quite striking, with golden-blonde hair, bright blue eyes, and a sprinkle of freckles on her nose.

"Thank you. I owned a spa when I lived in Miami and decided that I wanted to own one again when I moved here a few years ago. It's not too busy here, but I made this place into something that I absolutely love." The tone in her voice suggested that she really didn't care if she didn't have many clients. She loved her spa.

"It's perfect. We were hoping to have some girl time today. Can we each get a pedicure?" Bella noticed that Ivy was alone in the spa, so she doubted there were other clients waiting.

"Not a problem, I have three spa pedicure chairs in the room over here on the right. Come on back."

Ivy led them into the first room off a long, narrow hallway. The room, painted in an ocean-blue color, looked like a beach. Upon entering, Bella could hear the sounds of seagulls and waves crashing. The room even smelled like the ocean. Each passing moment, Bella became even more impressed. This place was perfection. It was such a shame that it wasn't full of people enjoying it.

"I'll start the water and add some herbal green-tea soak. This will help to get rid of any impurities," Ivy told them as she went about her work, filling the tubs and getting the chairs ready for them. Bella, Jessica, and Alyssa took off their shoes, rolled up their jeans, and sat in the soft chairs. They all moaned loudly as the massage chairs started working their magic. The jets rubbed their feet, and the scent of green tea slowly rose in the air.

"Who would like to go first?" Ivy asked, standing in front of the row of chairs. "Let Bella go first. This was her amazing idea," Alyssa said, looking over at Bella.

Ivy smiled and walked over to Bella. Sitting on the stool, she pulled herself up to the basin where Bella's feet were soaking in heaven.

"What brings you ladies here into our little Coltmann County?" Ivy asked. Of course, she would be curious. Everyone knew that they were new. It was as if they had that new-car scent all over them.

"Our car broke down a few days ago. The parts will be here Monday, so we might be leaving next week," Bella said, feeling a little sad but knowing she was going to be having a lot of girl talk in front of Ivy, she might as well just jump into it.

"Wow, you all must be on quite an adventure." Ivy was smiling at Bella as she started removing the old nail polish.

"Yeah, we came here to have a girls' day because we, or should I say that I, met some men." Bella said the last part of the sentence quickly, not sure what Ivy's reaction might be at hearing the word "some."

Ivy started laughing, obviously knowing that Bella was talking about multiple men. "You don't have to be shy or embarrassed. This is a community full of ménage couples. I'm married to Winston and Zane Weston, brothers, of course. They own the only hardware-slash-feed store in town. You're not going to get any judgment from me," Ivy told them all. She was proud to claim two men. It was clear in her voice. She didn't care what anyone thought. She was married to them both and happy.

"How does that work exactly? I mean, who do you marry? How can you choose, or do they choose?" Bella was asking so many questions she was sure that she was babbling. Jessica and Alyssa were both listening, probably wanting to know the same answers. This whole town seemed to be separated from reality. It didn't seem like it could exist.

"Well, I'm sure it works differently for different people. In my relationship, I married Winston. He's the oldest. That was really the only reason I married him over Zane. I was living in Miami and came here to visit my sister Chelsea a few years ago. I needed a vacation. Anyway, I was having dinner at the café when these two sexy men walked right up to my booth and sat down." Ivy laughed a little to herself as if she was remembering that moment. "From that moment, I knew that I never wanted to leave. I fell in love right away. I moved here the next week. I was completely compulsive."

That story told Bella a lot. If Ivy hadn't given them a chance, she wouldn't be married or have this beautiful spa.

Bella smiled, shaking her head in agreement. "Thank you for telling us your story." Bella took a deep breath. "I met three men, Clint, Clay, and Cody Colton." Bella waited for Ivy to acknowledge what she said. She still wasn't sure if Ivy was going to react negatively or not.

"Bella, I'm serious. I already told you my story. Now it's your turn," Ivy said, soothing her fears once more.

"You're right. I met the Colton brothers only a few days ago. I'm feeling really confused. I want to believe them, that I'm the one for them all. I just have some fears. I don't know if I can move here, but I know that I can't get into the car and leave them, either. I don't want to end something that could be wonderful." Bella took a deep breath and relaxed further into the chair.

"I know the Colton brothers. They're good men. Most men in this town are looking for a woman that they can share. That might seem easy, but think about it, especially with the three Coltons. They have different personalities, likes and dislikes, and of course, different tastes in women. Add that all up, and to be honest, you must be quite amazing to have all three of them wanting you," Ivy explained. She applied the mango peel to Bella's feet and moved to Alyssa to get her pedicure started.

"Bella…when we were walking here, you said you had an idea. What is it? Why do you need Jess and I?" Alyssa opened her eyes and looked at Bella, waiting patiently.

"One major block in my way is the fact that I don't have a job. We all work so well together, I thought it would be amazing if we could do something, like open a store." Bella stopped but continued quickly before Jessica or Alyssa could say anything. "Jessica has that amazing online store. She does great designs. We could start there, making an actual store and still doing online orders. We could sell her lingerie designs and some other unique items. Bath stuff, jewelry, maybe even some sex toys." Bella finally stopped and looked over at her friends, who were looking at her with a mixture of shock and excitement. Maybe her idea wasn't so bad after all.

"Holy shit! You've been doing some serious thinking." Alyssa stared at Bella with a twinkle in her eyes. "I think that is the best idea ever! I can see it now. The storefront window could be a mixture of different items, and obviously, we want it aimed at both men and women, since, let's face it, men loving buying their woman sexy things." Alyssa was obviously on board, and Bella couldn't seem to contain her happiness either. The only real roadblock now was Jessica, and she was always a tough sell.

Ivy applied the mango peel to Alyssa and was moving over to Jessica when she added, "That sounds great. I like the way you think, Bella. I own the storefront next door. If you're serious, I'd be more than happy to sell to you ladies."

Bella sat up straighter now, loving Ivy more each passing moment she was in her presence. This could actually happen. She'd had the idea for a while, but never voiced it to Jessica or Alyssa, thinking it was somewhat silly. They all had gone into different career paths, Jessica into clothing and lingerie design, Alyssa into business management, and of course, Bella went to work in the nonprofit sector after getting her degree in psychology. This might be the perfect time for their dreams to come true.

Bella and Alyssa waited to hear what Jessica had to say. After all, they wanted to sell her designs. When Ivy returned to her chair to rinse the mango peel and continue the pedicure, Bella realized that several minutes had passed. They were all sitting in silence.

Ivy took off the peel and started to rub Bella's feet. "This is a moisture-lotion mixture of papaya and green tea. I made it. I usually make all my products. I don't sell them, though it would be pretty amazing to have a store where women could buy all-natural products."

Bella started laughing. Ivy knew just what to say all the time. "Ivy, I just want you to know that you are amazing. I have no idea how you got into this business, because you should be a therapist or something."

Alyssa started laughing as well, but Jessica stayed silent. She hadn't said one word the whole time. She listened intently to what they were saying, but didn't make a single comment.

Bella was starting to get a bad feeling when Jessica finally said, "That would be a huge change, not just for me, but for us all. It's such a good idea, though, Bella. I've thought about having a store for a while. Doing the online sales with the store could probably support us. It's a lot to think about. The cost to buy the store, any cost to refurbish, and of course, I don't want to leave Diana unemployed."

"I have some money in savings. I'm more than happy to empty it to start the store. I think that Ivy, our newest best friend, will sell it at a fair price." Bella looked at Ivy, gave a little wink and smile. "Alyssa is finished with school. She's great with numbers, and she could be in charge of the books. I'm sure any money she has, she'll add to mine. We can all be equal partners." Bella looked at Alyssa and waited for her to agree. At her nod, Bella continued. "Diana is more than welcome to come out here and join us. She won't lose her job. She only needs to relocate, and we can help her." Bella shifted in her chair to look directly at Jessica. "I know this is a huge step, but we can do this. I know this store will be a success."

"You're probably right. Before we make this huge decision, though, we need to go over the numbers. We need to find out where we stand financially. I don't want us to break the bank to make this happen, only to fail. We need to plan. Luckily, we have some time to talk more. I also need to talk to Diana, although I'm pretty sure she would move." Jessica smiled at her friends. "Ivy, when we're done, will you take us next door so we can check it out?"

"Absolutely. I've had the place a while. It's in good condition, though, so don't worry. I'm sure you won't spend much to get it ready for opening. Maybe a few cans of paint. With all the men around, I'm sure you'll also get the labor for free." Ivy laughed. She continued to work on the pedicures, and they started talking about all their ideas of how to make the perfect store.

* * * *

Ivy led Bella, Jessica, and Alyssa next door to the place that she hoped would be something amazing. More women coming into town and having more stores that catered to them would keep them around and, hopefully, happily spending money. Ivy unlocked the door, turned on the light, and patiently waited for a response. This would make the perfect store. It was an open space, with white shelves lining one wall. There was also a front counter, where a cash register could go. In the back, there was an office and a bathroom. The windows were huge, letting in plenty of natural light but also allowing people to see all the great things inside as well.

Ivy had bought the place because she wanted to be able to pick the people who would be sharing a wall with her. She planned to sell it to Bella, Jessica, and Alyssa when she heard what Bella's plan was. They wanted unique things, and with them selling her products, she could get more business. They could help each other. This just might work, but it seemed as though Jessica was the one who made the final decision.

"Well, take a look around and let me know what you think. I'm willing to sell it for what I paid for it. I'm not looking to make a profit." She stepped back and let them look around.

* * * *

Bella was impressed. The store was in great condition. They were going to have to do some cleaning and add a fresh coat of paint, but other than that, they could open the store quickly. That meant they could start making money rather than spending it. Jessica had to see that as well.

"Ivy, let's talk gravy. How much are you willing to sell this place to us for?" Bella decided to get all the information before they got too excited and couldn't move forward. "I think it's perfect. It won't take much work to get the store ready and open. I know that Jessica has some reservations, but Alyssa and I are really excited about this." Bella said a prayer and hoped that this would work out.

"I'm willing to sell it for what I paid for it. I bought it specifically to sell it to people that I wanted to have as neighbors." Ivy smiled at them. "I've been hoping to have more girl friends. Having a girls' night alone is absolutely no fun." She made a funny face, and Bella laughed. "If you all moved here, it would be great to plan karaoke nights, poker parties, and even the occasional shopping outing. I'm more than willing to set up a payment plan, but real estate here really isn't that expensive. Hold your breath…sixty-four thousand dollars." Ivy bit her bottom lip. She looked a bit nervous, and Bella wanted to give her the answer she was looking for.

Bella turned toward her friends with a huge smile. The price was definitely lower than she had thought. Compared to her, she knew that Jessica had assumed a lot more—especially if the look on Jessica's face was any indication. Her mouth was slightly open as she turned around and looked at the building that would soon belong to them. Everything was starting to look up.

"Jessica, if I had to guess what you're thinking from the look on your face, I'd say you thought this was going to cost way more." Bella waited patiently for Jessica to say something.

"Absolutely. I'm a little shocked, to say the least. I guess I was expecting California prices. This might work out." Jessica turned to face her friends. "Don't get your hopes too high. I need to talk to Diana and figure out how we're going to move all our stuff here, where we're going to stay. We might need to rent a house for a while." Jessica was always the planner. She never just jumped into anything, but at least this was a step in the right direction.

"All right, Ivy, we want to keep this quiet for a while. Just in case it doesn't work out, I don't want everyone in town expecting us to stay." Bella really didn't want Clint, Clay, or Cody to think she was staying, at least not yet. She still needed to figure out if this relationship was going to work. Adding more complications right now wasn't something she wanted to do.

"No problem. We can talk more about it later. If you have any questions, just let me know. I've got to head back to the spa now. I have a massage scheduled for Susan in a few minutes." Ivy led them out of the building, locking it up behind her.

Bella, Jessica, and Alyssa headed to the work truck and back to the guesthouse. They needed to have some privacy to discuss the possibilities, and a few phone calls needed to be made as well.

* * * *

Watching Bella walk away with her friends had been hard, but Clint knew that they needed to have a talk as well. He walked out of the café and headed over to the grocery store with Clay, Cody, Beau, and Chase. This might be their only opportunity to talk before the women finished their spa treatments. He was glad that Bella was feeling more at home here in Coltmann County, but he wanted her to be here with them always. They needed a plan to make this work.

"I can't believe their car is going to be fixed this week. Jeez, right when we find her, and she might be leaving us." Clay said with a disappointed tone. "We can't force her to stay. I'm not even sure we can ask her. She does have family, friends, and other obligations in California." Clay was talking aloud but not to anyone in particular.

"Well, hopefully, if we can all put our heads together, we might come up with a great plan," Cody said.

"I say we head over to the pub, talk to Justin and Grant, and get them involved as well. I think all of us want them to stay. We might as well involve them," Beau suggested as they walked down Main Street.

As a single unit, they walked across the street and headed toward the pub. The grocery shopping would have to wait.

The pub was closed, although Justin and Grant were always around since the whole top floor was their home. It was a nice, large building. The back door was usually unlocked, because most people didn't lock their doors. The men walked around the building, toward the back, looking forward to having some time that they wouldn't be interrupted, and could talk.

When they opened the door, Justin was behind the bar, and Grant was sitting at a table with a huge pile of paperwork. "Afternoon, gentlemen, something we can help you with?" Justin started grabbing beers from the cooler and opening them, setting them on the bar.

Clint walked over to the bar and was reminded of how they met and grew up together in Coltmann County. Justin and Grant were brought here when they were just boys. The original owners of the bar had adopted them, since they couldn't have children. Unfortunately, they had died in a car accident a couple years back. They were both still struggling with the loss of them. They had different last names by choice, Grant Hollis for their dad Thomas, and Justin Truman for their dad Timothy. They escaped the sadness and joined the military, only coming back when they were ready for a home and a family.

"Thanks, Justin, Grant, how are you guys this afternoon?" Clint took the leadership position and started things off. Everyone else seemed to be lost in thought. The idea of the women leaving left them all a bit worried and sad. "We came to talk about Bella, Jessica, and Alyssa." He wanted to put all the cards on the table. They didn't have much time, although he really wasn't sure how long pedicures took.

"What about Alyssa?" Grant finally stood up from the table. He hadn't really acknowledged them until that moment. He walked over to the bar, nodded at Justin, and sat down. Justin opened a beer for him and slid it down. He sat their silently, waiting for his question to be answered. Grant was the silent one. He didn't communicate often. The fact that he asked about Alyssa meant he cared. This was a good sign, Clint thought.

"Well, the parts were ordered for their car and should be here Monday. Beau and I will probably be able to get it fixed soon after," Chase told them. "They're leaving next week. We don't know if there is a way to stop them."

They all were silent for a few minutes, obviously thinking. Clint waited, wondering what the others were thinking. Unsure of what next week would bring, this was the first time in a long time that there was someone he was excited about having a future with.

"Well, the only thing we can do is to try to convince them that they want to stay. Show them how much we want them, and that we can take care of them. Maybe even show them what job opportunities are here if they want to work. I know Alyssa is great when it comes to business. She has her degree in business management. She'd do a hell of a lot better than me when it comes to this bar," Grant told them.

Clint was taken back for a moment. In such a short amount of time, Alyssa had obviously gotten under Grant's skin. She made him smile, something he hadn't done in a while. It shouldn't be surprising, though, since she was such a little spitfire, not willing to take any crap from anybody. She was a bit bossy but also caring and funny and had a ton of energy. Clint hoped that something would happen with them.

"We've been giving Bella a lot of love and attention. I think she's actually unsure if she wants to leave. When she talks about leaving, I can see sadness in her eyes. This whole situation has been a bit hard on her emotionally," Clay said to everyone.

Clint knew everything was happening a little too fast for Bella. She was uncertain of her role, if this would actually work out with them, and then, of course, of saying good-bye to her friends. They were a tight family unit, and being without them would really kill her.

"They all need to stay, though. Otherwise, I feel like Bella will leave, if only for them. She wants us, she wants to be with us, but at the same time, she doesn't want to be without Jessica or Alyssa." Clay said.

"Getting Jessica and Alyssa to stay, that's going to be tough," Cody interjected. "Clint and Clay are right. Bella is already ours. She wants to stay, but she doesn't want her friends leaving. Do you guys want Alyssa and Jessica to stay?"

Chase, Beau, Justin, and Grant all spoke at once. "Of course."

"Yes."

Well, at least they were all in this together. Seven against three, not bad odds, except the three were the ones who really held all the power. Even as Clint thought that last part, he was able to crack a half smile and give an inward laugh. Those three women had them all so wrapped up.

"We're all in this together, gentlemen. Tomorrow we'll have the barbecue and introduce the women to everyone in town. Everyone will welcome them, and we all make sure that they are getting lots of love and attention. The goal is to make sure they don't want to leave town. Find out what their goals are, just as Grant said, and help them achieve their goals, if we can. Whatever they can do in California, they can do here in Texas." Clint thought he had it all figured out. They were going to work together. Those women had no idea what they were in for, and they weren't going to give up.

"All right. Beau and I will really focus our attentions on Jessica. We have made a lot of progress. We just need more time, and time isn't on our side. Justin and Grant can decide what they're going to do. I'm not discussing my plan with any of you, though. It's between Beau and me." Chase wasn't going to budge, and Clint knew that he was a strong man and wouldn't say a thing about Jessica.

"You're right. It isn't anyone else's business. I'm not planning to share our personal life or details either. Keep everything to yourselves. I can respect that." Clint nodded at Chase and Beau, understood how they felt. He wasn't going to share his relationships or any details with anyone but Bella and his brothers.

"Well, we've got to go buy supplies for the barbecue tomorrow. I also want to head back to the ranch and see if we can convince Bella to come horseback riding with us on a tour of the ranch. We had better head out. Bella's probably done with her appointment already. I want to make sure we have lots of time with her. Every minute counts when we're running out of time." Clint stood up and motioned to Clay and Cody. They all headed toward the back door. They had a few things to do before they met up with their lovely Bella.

"Grant and I will bring beer tomorrow. We can all start our

missions to keep our women." Justin laughed as Grant shook his head. They were complete opposites. It was going to take an amazing woman to understand and love them both, Clint thought. Justin and Grant went back to work as the rest of them left the pub to do various errands.

* * * *

Bella, Jessica, and Alyssa were all at the guesthouse, relaxing and going over the details of their possible move, when they heard voices drifting in through the open windows. It was a warm, beautiful day. The sun was shining, and there was a nice breeze coming in to cool them off. When they had gotten to the house, they had poured some white wine over small chunks of ice, propped up their feet, and continued their rather intense conversation from the spa. They had been talking ever since, and so far, it seemed that a move could actually work out.

Jessica had called her assistant Diana right away to talk to her about the plan, to see if she wanted to move here or just continue to do part of the online business work from California. She didn't want to leave her unemployed, but after going over some numbers, Jessica thought the best thing to do was to rent a house and purchase the building. Leaving California would actually help them save money.

Diana was quite animated about the new opportunity. She immediately started packing up her things. She was ready to move, ready for a change. She also said she would help the moving company in packing up all their belongings. This meant that they might not have to go back to California to move all their things. They could take care of everything from here.

Alyssa called a moving company to talk about the cost of a move, including a full pack at all three of their homes. She also set up an appointment with the moving agency to meet with Diana. This was going to be a big process, and until it was confirmed, they all decided not to say anything to anyone. They were even able to convince Ivy not to say anything. She was going to be bringing the paperwork to the barbecue tomorrow. Not telling anyone, was a "just in case" factor.

Bella was so happy, though. The huge smile on her face was a dead giveaway. She wanted to run to Clint, Clay, and Cody and tell them how happy she was. She wanted to move her things into their house. She wanted to start their future together. She still needed to talk to her mom, though. That was really the only person who would miss her. They could still visit on holidays, and maybe eventually her mom could move here. That would be great, still being able to have mother-daughter days.

There was a knock on the door, and Bella got up to answer it, knowing it was probably her men. She had to remember to keep her mouth shut until everything was signed and ready to go. Although, they did need to find a house to rent, so maybe talking to them wouldn't be such a bad idea. Bella opened the door slowly and smiled when she saw Clay standing in front of her. Behind him, Clint and Cody were sitting on horses.

"Hello, stranger," Bella said. She leaned into Clay and kissed his lips. She took her time, kissing him slowly, opening her mouth to play with his tongue. It seemed like forever since she had been able to be this close to any of her men. Even though she had just seen them this morning, it felt like a lifetime.

"Did you have a nice appointment, baby? Show me those cute little toes." Clay was breathing a little harder. He obviously hadn't been expecting such a wonderful hello from her. Her kiss said everything she needed to say. She had missed them just as much as they missed her, and that felt good.

"Wonderful. Ivy is fantastic. I wish you would've told me about her sooner, and her spa, it's every girl's fantasy. We had the best time." Bella leaned down and slowly took off her sandals so she could give her men a better look. She was wearing a low-cut V-neck T-shirt and tight jeans. As she leaned over, she made sure the men got an even better look. When she heard a male groan, she knew it had worked like a charm. She was feeling flirty and sexy. Maybe it was the wine, or maybe it was the fact that she was moving here. Either way, she was satisfied, her life felt complete, and she was at peace with her decision to move. It was going to be tough to keep this secret.

"Baby, we packed a picnic, thought maybe you would join us for a ride around the ranch. We even brought you your own horse." Cody got off his horse and headed toward the patio, where Clay was holding Bella close. "Come and meet her. She's one of the sweetest horses we own. Her name is Gracie." Cody held out his hand and waited until Bella grabbed hold.

She followed him over to meet a beautiful jet-black horse with a white underbelly and neck. She was saddled and ready for a ride. Clint was still sitting on his huge horse, looking at Bella, waiting to see her reaction. In fact, they seemed to be worried she might not join them on the evening ride they planned.

"She's fantastic. I'd love to go for a ride. One problem, I don't have my tennis shoes, probably not a good idea to ride in sandals." Bella was a bit disappointed.

"No problem, baby. Clint can you hand me Bella's shoes?" Clay walked over and grabbed her shoes from his brother. One thing about the Colton brothers was that they were always prepared. They had prepared for any excuses.

Bella gifted him with a smile and another kiss. He was definitely on her good list today. "I'll tell Jessica and Alyssa that I'm leaving. Should I also tell them not to wait up?" Bella smiled and waited for an answer. She wasn't planning to come back here tonight. Nope, she was staying with her men.

Clint smiled and gave a slight groan. "No, baby, tell them you'll be coming home with us. We promise to take good care of you." He winked at her, and Bella felt her cheeks burn a little. That one sentence had so many meanings.

Bella turned to see Jessica and Alyssa standing on the patio, watching them. They were both whispering to each other.

"We heard. Go ahead. Have some fun. We'll see you tomorrow at the barbecue. What time, Clint?" Alyssa was ready to push Bella out the door and into their arms.

Bella heard Jessica whisper, "At least someone's getting some."

Alyssa shook her head and laughed quietly as they shared their little joke that they thought nobody heard.

"Well, ladies, you're more than welcome to come to the ranch house whenever you like. People will probably show up around one o'clock to start drinking and snacking. We have a huge game room, with darts, pool table, and ping-pong. Outside, we have horseshoes. Those games get pretty serious with the folks around here." While Clint talked, Bella, Jessica, and Alyssa shared differing looks of surprise on their faces. It was funny to hear Clint go on about the seriousness of these games. It became even more serious when picking teams.

Before he could continue, Bella interrupted, "Okay, time for us to go. I'll see you both tomorrow around one. Have a good night. If you run out of wine, you should head to the pub." Bella winked at Alyssa when she said "pub."

Alyssa didn't want to hear about Justin and Grant. She was being tight-lipped when it came to them.

Bella kept thinking back to the night she left her there at the pub and wondered what could've happened. Did they hook up? Did they walk her to the motel? Did Alyssa leave the pub upset? Those were the questions Bella hoped to ask soon. Maybe she could get some answers on the next girls' night.

Clay and Cody helped Bella get on Gracie, and they slowly headed away from the guesthouse.

# Chapter 11

Clint was so happy to have Bella back with them again. As they headed out toward the far east side of the ranch. He really wanted to show Bella the lake they had there. He wanted to show her the spot he went to when he needed to be alone or to think. He wanted her to love this place as much as they did, although he felt like she was almost to that point already. She looked around as they rode, talking joyously about everything she saw. Looking at everything now, through her eyes, made him appreciate this place more. Whatever had happened today had put her in a great mood.

"You liked the spa?" Clint asked, wanting to know more about their talk, but not really wanting to ask the question. He didn't want to seem nosy.

"It was perfect. The whole atmosphere was just unbelievable. Ivy is great, too. She's super smart. Seriously, she should be a therapist." Bella smiled.

"We're glad you had a good time with your girlfriends. We don't want your friends thinking we're trying to monopolize all your time, sweetie." Clay pulled his horse close to her so that their knees were touching. He did that often, came close to just touch her. She enjoyed their attention and affection. It made her feel so special and loved. They rode together, in a tight group. The horses didn't seem to mind being so close either.

"Ivy is great, and so are her husbands, Winston and Zane. They'll be here tomorrow. We helped them gut and refurbish that building she's in. They were working on it during the weekends and when they had some free time. We helped them so that she could start her business faster." Cody could see that Bella was interested in learning more about the town.

"That's impressive. You guys must be really handy. The place looks great. I hope that when I'm ready to move into a place, there are handy men like you around." Bella looked like she wanted to say more, but she stopped and looked around. Clint looked over at her, wanting to push her to keep talking, but he left it alone.

"We'll always be around to help you, baby," Clay said as he bumped his knee into her to get her attention. When Bella looked over, he said, "We want to help you with anything you might need."

"Your land is so beautiful. I can see why you love it here. The fresh air, the openness, it's peaceful. We don't really have any space like this where I'm from." Bella looked around her. Clint knew what she saw. There was nothing but open land as far as the eye could see, rolling hills, tall grass, and huge trees. A gentle breeze was blowing, and the only sounds were coming from the horses. This was paradise.

"We love it here. It was nice to travel a little, with the rodeo circuit, but it felt even better to come home," Cody said from the other side of Bella. They were getting closer to the spot they wanted to stop and have a picnic, maybe swim a little, and learn more about their beautiful Bella.

"The perfect place for our picnic is just over that hill. We'll be there in a couple of minutes," Clint told Bella. He could tell that she wasn't used to riding, but she sat up straight like a pro. Just looking at her, surrounded by them, everything felt right. He was plagued with doubts, though, even as he smiled at her. Every minute they had with her, he wanted to be perfect, so that when the time came, maybe she wouldn't get in the car and drive away.

They rode in a comfortable silence, enjoying the scenery and just being close to each other. Bella looked at all three of them. They were so amazing. It was hard to believe that these men could think that she was the one for them.

"Whoa, this is the spot we wanted to bring you to, Bella. Sit tight.

I'll come over and help you down." Clint dismounted and walked over to Bella. Holding Gracie's reins, he picked Bella up and put her gently on the ground. Clint pulled her close and leaned down to take possession of her lips. He ate at her mouth like a starving man, enjoying her taste. It felt like he hadn't kissed her in days, instead of a matter of hours. While he intensified their kiss, Bella leaned closer to him, making sure their bodies were touching everywhere, and he groaned in her mouth.

Clay and Cody moved around behind her, but Clint refused to stop kissing her soft lips. He was holding her in his arms, and his body wrapped around hers in a protective hold. It felt so good to be there. This is where she belonged.

"Bring her over to the blanket so we can help pleasure our woman." Clay's voice finally was able to break through the fog. Clint gave her a few more tender kisses on her lips, then neck, guiding her backward toward Clay and Cody.

Bella kept her eyes closed and Clint guided her toward the blanket. He turned her around, and she was met with the astounding sight of two gorgeous, naked men. She groaned and put her hands out to touch them.

"Not so fast, sweetheart," Clint whispered in her ear as he pinned her hands to her sides. "We are going to strip you, lick you, and touch you. It will be your turn soon, but we go first." Clint laughed softly when Bella squirmed and tried to get out of his tight grip. She wanted to get to Clay and Cody.

"Please. Please let me touch them. They're so sexy," Bella whispered to Clint. She was so excited and horny. She needed them.

"It's okay, baby, you'll get your chance to do anything you want to them. Trust me. But first, Clay and Cody get their turn. I'll hold her arms. Come and get her." Clint encouraged his brothers to seduce their woman. He wanted to watch her receive pleasure. It made his cock turn hard just thinking about them touching her.

Bella started moaning before they even touched her. Having Clint restrain her movements turned her on and made her pussy drip with anticipation. She watched from hooded eyes as Clay and Cody approached her. Their cocks were both hard, and she could see clear fluid dripping from them both. With Clint standing behind her, Clay came straight toward her, and Cody completed the circle.

Clay swooped down to capture her mouth with his. His hands on her bottom pulled her close. His mouth took control of hers, filling her with the taste and heat of his. His firm lips moved on hers, and she automatically leaned against him. Her movements were still restrained as she tried to get closer. Cody started stripping her. He didn't move slowly. Instead, he ripped, pulled, and grabbed.

Bella squirmed, trying to pull free of Clint. She wanted to get naked faster, and she was so wet.

"Are you going to listen to us, baby? I'll let your arms go, but you have to promise to be a good girl." Clint knew she was horny. It was obvious. Her body was flushed, and her moans and gasps filled the air.

"Yes, yes, anything. I need Clay." Bella continued to kiss Clay as Cody started rubbing her naked body.

Clint let go of Bella's arms, stepping back so that Clay could get closer. Clay lifted her. She wrapped her legs around his waist and squirmed to get closer. The feel of his chest against her breasts, and his tight stomach against her mound, had her rubbing against him.

When he lifted his head, his eyes glowed. His lips twitched before he leaned down to nip her bottom lip. "You really are perfect for us. I love the way you rub against me when you're aroused. I don't think I could ever get enough of you, love." He dropped a hard kiss on her mouth and lowered them both onto the soft blanket.

Clay started kissing her down her throat, nibbling her neck, and moving toward her waiting breasts. Every time he touched them, Bella would shriek, and her nipples would harden instantly. They were quite sensitive. He moved his body off hers so that his brothers could have access to her body.

Cody touched his fingers to her folds, parting them and kneeling down between her thighs. He was waiting for Clay to move to the side so that he could go after her pussy.

Clint ran a hand down her body. “Get her nice and wet. We don’t have lube, and I want to watch you take her ass. Would you like that, love? Cody’s going to fuck that tight ass while I watch, and Clay is going to take that hot pussy.”

Jesus, the way they talked aroused her so much. She started thrashing and cried out in surprise and pleasure when a large finger thrust into her pussy.

Cody chuckled. “She’s already nice and wet. I’m just going to get her ass ready. Clay, lay down and let Bella straddle you. I’m going to stretch her ass.”

Clay lay down and pulled Bella onto of him. “Don’t let her impale her pussy on your cock yet. She’s too anxious. I don’t want this to be over before it begins.” Cody held Bella still before she could go for Clay’s cock.

“Please. I need more.” Bella moaned and rubbed her body on Clay’s. His hands on her breasts drove her crazy as he plucked and pulled on her nipples.

Clay grabbed her hands and put them above her head. “Keep your hands right where they are. We need you to relax while Cody works on your tight ass, baby.”

Bella did what they told her as Cody licked her ass, getting her tight hole nice and wet. He used his fingers, gathering her own juices on his fingers. He started slowly with one finger, pumping it in and out of her ass. Bella began moving on his finger, shaking with need.

“Does my baby need a cock inside her ass? Let me get my cock nice and wet first.” With that, Cody surged into her pussy. Her cries got even louder as his thrusts deepened. She kept her arms where Clay had put them as Clay pinched her nipples.

“Oh God! Oh God! More!” Bella whimpered in frustration when Cody withdrew.

"Hang on, baby. I'm going to fuck your ass now. Clay, get ready. After I'm fully in her ass, I want you to take that perfect pussy." Cody sank slowly into her ass, not stopping until he was fully seated. He was breathing hard. Sweat slowly started dripping down his face. "This was the most amazing feeling, and I want it to last."

"Oh shit, I'm not going to last long. Clay…start fucking her." Cody slowly pulled out and pushed back in, setting up a good rhythm with Clay.

Bella held her breath, shaking with need as both Clay and Cody set up a slow, steady speed. She was so close. Oh God, could sex always be this good? Everything was perfect. She turned her head, looking at Clint.

"Baby, you look so sexy." Clint walked over. After watching Bella being pleasured, he wanted to be a part of it. He started rubbing her back and shoulder, leaning over to kiss her while she rode Clay.

Bella cried out as they filled her repeatedly, robbing her of every bit of the control she struggled to hang on to. "Yes. Ohh!" She couldn't believe how completely her body surrendered to them when they took her this way.

"I'm not going to last. Fuck. Clint, rub her clit. Make her come first." Cody was pumping into Bella so fast.

Clint flicked Bella's clit only once. That was all it took for her to go over. She screamed out her pleasure, shaking uncontrollably. She heard both Cody and Clay find their completion, but she was too far gone to pay attention. She felt hands rubbing her body. Clay was holding her close to his chest. Bella kept her eyes closed, and she caught her breath. She felt them pulling out of her body, and felt like mush.

Clint took Bella into his arms so he could hold her. She was so beautiful all flushed and relaxed. Cody and Clay got dressed in a daze. "Clay, can you get the picnic basket? Let's feed our beautiful Bella."

Clay pulled his pants on, still trying to breathe evenly. Being with

Bella was always so perfect. She wasn't afraid to show them her passion. She wanted them just as badly as they wanted her. He opened the large basket they brought, filled with everything they could think of since they still weren't sure what she liked yet. He opened the fresh-fruit container first, sat next to Clint, who was holding Bella, and offered her a strawberry.

Bella opened her eyes to find Clay holding a beautiful strawberry to her lips. She gave him a small smile and took a bite. Clay fed Bella while she sat in Clint's lap, and Cody grabbed a sandwich and sat down next to them.

"Wow, that was amazing. I don't think I've ever come so hard in my life. I feel almost out of it afterward," Bella told them.

"Making love to you, it's always wonderful. Luckily, we can take care of you." Clay smiled down at her.

"This picnic was a great idea. Thank you for bringing me out here," Bella told them, and she meant it.

"After we eat, let's head back to the ranch. You can take a nice, relaxing bath," Cody suggested. Clint thought it was the best idea he'd ever heard. Having her in their large tub was always fun. Bella was so free and open. They needed as much time as possible to convince her that this was where she belonged.

"I'd love that. Are you going to join me?" Bella asked him with a giggle. She knew that he suggested the bath in hopes of joining her.

They all ate in relative silence, relaxing back on the blanket, enjoying just being together. When it started to get darker, Clint, Clay, and Cody helped Bella to get dressed. They all climbed onto their horses and headed for home. Bella yawned deeply, and Cody stopped his horse next to hers and pulled her into his lap.

"It's okay, baby. Close your eyes and put your head on my chest." Clint had noticed Bella nodding off, so he was glad the Cody reacted so fast and pulled her onto his lap before she completely fell asleep. Clay grabbed Gracie's reins and followed them toward the ranch.

* * * *

Bella hadn't realized how tired she was until she woke up in Cody's arms. He was handing her off to Clay, who was waiting to take her. She went to Clay, and he walked into the house.

"Do you want to take a bath, baby? You would probably feel a lot better, waking up clean in the morning." Clay headed toward the master bedroom, and the bath that was waiting for her.

Clint was waiting for her in the bathtub. He'd decided to get the water started and then thought it would be better to join her instead of watch. He made sure the water was nice and warm. He even added some vanilla-scented bath salts for her. He wanted Bella to be completely relaxed before they went to bed.

Clay walked in and saw him sitting in the tub. He gave Clint a smile and a raised eyebrow in question. He knew Clint was crazy for Bella just like the rest of them. In fact, Clint probably fell in love with Bella that first night at the café.

"Look who's waiting for you, baby," Clay whispered to Bella.

Clint had given both Clay and Cody the afternoon with her. Now he wanted to be alone with their woman. He had watched this afternoon, and now he was desperate for some one-on-one time.

"Clint needs some of your attention, baby." Clay added.

Clint held out his arms and moved to the side of the tub when Clay walked in with Bella. "I'll take care of her. Why don't you and Cody go shower, and we'll meet you in bed."

Clay kissed Bella's head and winked at her, handing her off to Clint. Clay headed out of the bathroom, leaving them alone.

Bella snuggled close to Clint. She loved being in his arms. It felt right. She started kissing his chest, licking him, when she felt him hold her tighter. She began to feel more aggressive. She turned her body to straddle him, kissing his neck, moving up to his full lips.

Clint groaned when he felt Bella touching him and kissing his chest. She knew him so well. He really needed some attention from her. Especially after watching his brothers love her today, he wanted to be deep inside her pussy. He let her take charge, doing whatever she wanted. He used every ounce of restraint he had, keeping his hands on her hips when he was tempted to play with her body.

"I want your cock in my pussy, Clint. Take me." Bella needed him. She had no patience for any kind of foreplay. She wanted to feel his cock pounding her pussy.

"Tell me what you want, baby. I'll do whatever you want." Clint loved hearing her talk dirty. Her voice turned from sweet and innocent to smoky. She whispered the dirty words. It was so cute, like she couldn't say them loud.

"I want you to lean me over the tub and put your cock in my pussy. I want you to fuck me really hard." Bella could feel his cock getting harder. She was rubbing her body against his, feeling his sparse chest hair tickle her. Her nipples were hard, and she was moving up and down, trying to get his cock into her pussy. She kept talking, though, wanting him to take her. "I want you to hold my hair in your hand tightly, and I want your other hand holding my hip." She moaned into his ear. This dirty talk was making her wetter.

She closed her eyes thinking about it, what he would do, as she continued to rub her breasts against his chest. Clint hadn't said anything yet, but she could tell his control was slowly breaking. He was breathing harder and groaning every time her pussy touched his cock.

Clint let her be in charge for another minute, enjoying her body moving against his. After listening to her whisper what she wanted, he was ready to pound nails his cock was so hard and ready for her. He wanted to claim her in the most primitive way, mark her, and make sure she knew whom she belonged to.

Moving quickly, Clint held her tight, turning her and pushing her against the side of the tub. Using his left forearm, he held her down, and using his right hand, he guided his cock to her pussy. With one hard stroke, he sank deep inside her luscious body. He didn't give

Bella time to adjust. He just started pounding his cock into her. Her words had affected him, broken his control, and he fucked her harder and harder. Clint moved his hands to where wanted them, making sure she felt his power. If she wanted to submit, then he planned to master her body.

Bella couldn't even think. She knew Clint would react soon, but she wasn't prepared to want to submit so completely to him. He had one hand in her hair, holding her head tightly. With his other hand, he massaged her hip and ass, moving his large fingers closer to her dark hole.

"Oh God, please, Clint, I need more." Bella groaned deep in her throat. She moved her ass to get closer to his roaming fingers.

Clint slapped her ass hard to prevent her from moving. Bella moaned louder, her voice echoing in the large bathroom. Their baby loved to be fucked hard, and he was going to give her everything she wanted and more. Clint felt her juices flowing down his cock. That spank had made her wetter. He'd have to tell his brothers. Clint held her hair tighter and smacked her ass again. Seeing his handprint appear made him feel more possessive.

"Oh, baby, I'm going to give you everything you want." Clint was gritting his teeth. Her pussy felt like heaven. He never wanted to leave.

"Oh God, Clint, please shove your finger in my ass." Bella was becoming even more vocal, and she didn't even care. She was close. Never in her life had she felt so connected to another human being. She wasn't leaving them—that was her last thought as she felt Clint shove his large finger into her ass. She shrieked and started coming, shaking and crying.

Clint felt Bella come and immediately fucked her harder and deeper, until he felt his balls draw up tight and felt the tingle at the bottom of his spine. He held her hips tight with both hands and came on a loud groan. Clint put his head on her back, kissing her lightly. He was still feeling the aftershocks of his orgasm when he heard Clay and Cody come into the bathroom.

Clay and Cody rubbed Bella's back and arms, soothing her and calming her while Clint slowly pulled. He still held her to him, though, kissing her and rubbing his hands on the red handprints that were disappearing. Clint smiled at his brothers, knowing that they had been standing just outside the door, listening to Bella come. She was magnificent, honest in her reactions and honest about what satisfied her. It was such an amazing experience making love to a woman who wasn't afraid to voice what she wanted.

"Come on, baby, let's get you to bed. Clint will meet us there," Clay said over his shoulder to Clint. It looked like tonight would be him and Cody holding Bella.

Clay and Cody helped Bella from the tub, drying her off with fluffy white towels. Then they walked her to the bed and tucked her in. Before her head even touched the pillow, she was gently snoring. Cody and Clay got into bed on either side of her, pulling her close so that they could hold her.

Bella moved around until she was comfortable, and on a quiet whisper, she said, "I love you."

Her statement of love wasn't directed toward anyone specific, but both Clay and Cody heard her.

Clint let out a sigh. He loved hearing her say those three words. He was glad he hadn't missed it. He was now even more eager to keep her with them. "We should probably tell her tomorrow."

"Tell her what?" Cody looked up at Clint. He knew his brother was already in love with Bella. They all were. "That we love her?" Cody rubbed Bella's neck as he kissed her cheek.

"Yeah. Maybe if we tell her we love her, she might stay, knowing that we do want a relationship. Hell, maybe we should just ask her to marry us." Clay knew he might be jumping the gun a bit, but time was short, and they needed Bella to realize how serious this was for them.

"I'm on board with that." Cody added his thoughts to the mix.

"Me, too. So, we get Grandma's ring out of the safe tomorrow and ask her." Clint decided that was probably the best idea. Just tell Bella how they felt. It hadn't been that long, but she had to realize how special this relationship was. He said a silent prayer as he got on the bed and rubbed Bella's feet. "Please, please say yes."

"We didn't use condoms this last time we were with Bella. I didn't even think about until I was cleaning up the horses. Clay and I talked about it. That's why we were standing outside the door. Did you use one?" Cody was really worried. He had wanted to talk to Bella, but she fell asleep too fast. The three of them wanted children, but what if Bella didn't want any? He didn't want her to have regrets. They would have to talk about it in the morning.

"No, I didn't. After she whispered her dirty story, I never thought to grab one. I hope she's not too upset when she wakes up." Clint put his head on Bella's thigh and said a little prayer before falling asleep. "Please, please don't leave us."

Clint went to sleep rubbing Bella's leg. This is the way he wanted each night to end, with Bella in their bed, holding her close.

# Chapter 12

Bella woke up alone. She lay in bed, quietly stretching, and thinking about her men. Yes, her men, she finally wanted to yell it, to tell everyone and anyone that Clint, Clay, and Cody belonged to her. She wanted to find them and tell them she wasn't leaving Coltmann County.

Whenever she'd spent time with Clint, she always loved how adored she felt in his arms. Strong and masculine, he always made her feel so feminine and protected, as though nothing could happen to her. She felt sexy and innocent at the same time. He made her feel like the most amazing person in his world.

Cody made her feel wild, desired, and needed. He would spend time learning each part of her as though they hadn't been together, and it drove her wild. He would always hold her afterward until the trembling stopped, and he would kiss her anywhere he could reach.

Clay always seemed different. Sometimes playful, sometimes more intense, usually gentle, their lovemaking filled her with a deep sense of well-being, as if she'd come home. He just liked being around her and touching her. Even if it was in passing, he would reach out.

She loved them all, and she planned on moving here and starting a career and possibly a family with the three of them. They hadn't used condoms, and although the reminder had been at the tip of her tongue, she had wanted to feel them completely. She was on birth control, though, but she should probably have that discussion today.

Bella got out of bed. She needed to find her men and talk about her move. It was time. She didn't want to wait for Jessica and Alyssa to make the announcement at the barbecue. They deserved to hear it from her.

Bella searched the house and couldn't find them. She looked through each room, yelling out their names. She decided to go outside to do a search for them. When she opened the door, she was greeted with the sight of people all around. It looked like people were arriving early for this afternoon's party. There was a huge grill in the yard, tables were everywhere, and a dance floor was even being temporarily installed. This brought a completely new meaning to "backyard barbecue." This was an event.

Bella had to tell them. Even though she was dressed in a large T-shirt and boy shorts, she didn't want to wait any longer. She had woken up thinking about her men and the future, and she couldn't wait any longer. Bella walked out onto the patio, looking around, looking for any sign of Clint, Cody, or Clay. When she couldn't spot them immediately, she went searching.

"Morning, Bella, or should I say afternoon? The guys are in the barn." Chase was the first person she came across on her way to the barn. That was the first place she was planning on looking.

"Thanks, Chase, I was just headed there. I hadn't realized how late I'd slept. Although, you are early." Bella wished she had gotten dressed before coming outside to find them, but it was too late now. She had to keep moving.

"This isn't early, darlin'. Maybe you should get dressed before coming outside. Everyone can see your ass, sweet cheeks." Chase laughed back at Bella.

"Well, Chase, I had no idea you were checkin' my ass out," Bella said over her shoulder as she walked into a wall. Wait, no, it wasn't a wall. She looked up and into the face of a seriously pissed-off Clint.

"Good morning, honey, I was just looking for you. Is everything okay?"

Bella was concerned to see Clint so upset. She'd never seen any of them upset before.

"Why are you walking around in a T-shirt and panties? You don't even have shoes on, Bella. What's going on?" Clint was upset. She'd never heard him raise his voice. He was acting like a different man, and she realized how truly possessive he was. "Chase, why are you looking at Bella's ass? Isn't there something you should be doing?"

"I was just teasing her, Clint, no harm intended." Chase walked away, probably realizing that Clint was serious.

"Wait, you're upset about his comment? He wasn't serious, Clint. Jeez. I came out here to find you." Bella wanted to understand why he was so angry. She wanted to calm him down. Clint walked toward her, and Bella couldn't move. She felt frozen in place. He looked like a predator, which made her his prey. She wasn't sure what to do. Her heart pounded, and she was stuck between fear and pleasure. It was a strange combination.

Bella shrieked when Clint grabbed her and threw her over his shoulder. She wasn't expecting that reaction. All of a sudden, he lowered his shoulder to her stomach. He lifted her over it as he straightened, and strode to the house with Clay and Cody hot on his heels and Bella flung upside down over his shoulder.

Bella didn't say anything, frozen on Clint's shoulder. She then realized what was happening. "What the hell are you doing, Clint? Put me down right now, damn it."

A sharp slap on her bottom had her getting angrier. What the hell had gotten into Clint? "Have you lost your mind? Clint, put me down!" Bella couldn't even think straight as she hit Clint on his lower back, paying him back for the spanking. "Fuck!" she yelled. Clint landed another hard slap to her ass.

"You don't need to cuss, baby. It doesn't sound pretty coming out of that mouth," Clay told her.

When they reached the house, Cody held the door open then closed it securely behind them after Clint walked in with a kicking Bella over his shoulder. Clint didn't stop until he was in their room. He dropped Bella on the bed and stepped back, crossing his arms over his large chest. Bella got to her knees, hands on her hips, glaring at him. It looked like they were in a standoff and neither one was willing to back down.

"Why did you come outside flaunting yourself?" He sounded ridiculous, and Bella knew she needed to fight. She couldn't deal with them turning into jealous monsters. "You can't be serious. I came outside to find you. You're overreacting, Clint." Bella wanted to be reasonable, but she was losing her patience quick. "You know I didn't leave the house to *flaunt my body*." She used air quotes on "flaunt my body" to make a point. "You have to realize that doesn't sound right."

Bella took a deep breath and looked at Clay and Cody, who were standing behind Clint. She wanted them to say something but also knew that this was between her and Clint. They needed to work it out.

"Why did you come outside? What was so important that you couldn't put clothes on?" Clint started to pace in front of the bed.

"I don't know if it matters anymore." Bella shook her head, dropping her arms. "I deserve an apology. You overreacted."

"It does matter. Chase, and every other man out there, was checking out your ass."

"Who cares? I am here with you. They all know that. I went outside to find you. Chase told me where you were. I went to the barn. I wasn't doing anything inappropriate. I don't know if this relationship can work if you don't trust me." Bella was barely hanging on. She wanted to cry and yell. This wasn't the way things were supposed to happen this morning.

Clint kneeled in front of the bed, facing Bella. "I do trust you. I'm sorry. Watching Chase flirt with you, and you flirt back, crushed me. We only have a little while longer together, and I'm starting to panic, I guess." Clint pulled Bella to him and put his head on her chest.

"Clint, I came outside to tell you, Clay, and Cody…" She looked up at Clay and Cody watching them. She motioned for them to come over to them. With one hand, she rubbed Clint's head, brushing her fingers through his hair. She reached out her other hand as Clay and

Cody walked over to the bed. "I'm staying. I had already planned this with Jessica and Alyssa, but they didn't want to tell anyone yet. Not until we signed papers and got the details of the move settled."

"What?"

"Oh my gosh, that's great news, baby."

"Are you serious?"

All three of her men answered at once. They all looked at her, shock, excitement, and sheer happiness clear in their eyes.

"I wanted to tell you yesterday, but I promised, and then after last night, I realized that I couldn't leave. My heart would still be here, and I would be too sad. When I woke up, I needed to find you. We put together a plan when we were at the spa. Ivy saved the day," Bella said with a little laugh. "She's selling us the building next to hers for a great price, and we're going to open a store, the three of us." She bit her lip and waited to hear what they had to say.

"Oh, baby, I hope you can forgive me for my stupidity. I promise that nothing like that will ever happen again." Clint put his head back in her lap.

"I hope you're planning on moving in with us," Cody demanded.

Clay went over to the dresser, grabbed something, came back to the bed, and knelt down next to Clint. Cody followed his lead. "Baby, I hope you know that we love you. We want you to move in here with us. We want to marry you," Clay said as he elbowed Clint.

Clint pulled his head up. "I love you. I can't picture my life without you."

Cody smiled, sitting on the bed next to Bella. "We've been trying to figure out a way to get you to stay. I think that's why Clint overreacted. I love you, too, Bella. We all do, and we all want to marry you."

Bella started crying. This day had not gone as planned. She wanted to tell them this news and celebrate. She wasn't expecting them to ask her to get married. This felt fast, but this relationship felt right, too. It was the best relationship she had ever had. She had never felt this way before, in love.

"I love you, all of you, too. I want this to work. That's why I tried so hard to figure out how to stay here."

They all looked at Bella, holding her close to them. "Bella, will you marry us?" Clint asked.

They waited for her to answer, staring at her, and she knew exactly what she wanted. She had been hoping for the best but almost expecting the worst. She was the one, the one for them. They wanted forever with her. She had tears welling up in her eyes, and her lower lip was quivering.

"Don't cry, baby. We love you. I know we haven't had too much time together yet, but now we have forever," Clay told her.

Another voice came up the stairs, toward the bedroom, "Hello, boys, are you up there?" their mom yelled up the stairs. "Boys?" She was at the bottom of the stairs.

"Yeah, Mom, be down in a minute," Cody yelled back.

"Bella, we need an answer, I don't want to rush you, baby. I want to walk out of this room, knowing you belong to us."

"Yes…yes, I'll marry you," Bella whispered through silent tears. She was so happy. "I'm gonna be Bella Colton. Um…who am I marrying? I mean…I can't marry all three of you…right?" Shoot, she had more questions.

"Baby, we can talk more about that later. Whatever makes you happy. Usually, the oldest brother marries the woman on paper, but we'll all be married to you," Clay told her. To them it really didn't matter, as long as she would belong to them.

"Okay. I had better get dressed. I look like a mess, and I want to clean myself up before I meet your parents." Bella held out her hand, waiting for them to put the ring on her finger. When Clay handed the box to Clint, he opened the box slowly and showed her the ring. "Oh my God, it's so beautiful," she gasped.

"It belonged to our grandmother. We've been waiting for the right woman," Clint told her as he pulled the delicate antique platinum ring out of the box. “Each of the diamonds represents us, and the biggest in the middle is you. You are at the heart of this relationship, baby.” He put the ring on Bella’s finger as more tears seeped out of her eyes.

They surrounded her with their warmth, holding her close. She felt their strength and love. She dried her tears as she kissed them and held them close. “Thank you. I love you all so much. I’m so happy.” Bella sniffled, trying to get herself under control. Today started a new life, and her future finally felt like it was going in the right direction.

“You all have to leave now. I need to get showered and dressed. I can’t believe I’m meeting your parents today. Oh my God, what if they don’t like me?” She hadn’t thought of that before. She started to panic a little.

“Baby”—Clay pulled Bella into his arms—“that’s silly. We love you, so, of course, they’re going to love you, too.”

Her fear wasn’t necessary. They had already talked about Bella to their parents. That’s why they had come back sooner, knowing this relationship was serious.

“Go get ready. We’ll go down and talk to them. When you’re ready, meet us in the kitchen,” Cody told her. Listening to Bella freak out about meeting their parents was laughable. Cody grabbed Bella’s hand and pulled her toward the bathroom. She needed to get showered and dressed. They could get downstairs and keep their parents occupied.

“Okay, I’m going.” Bella laughed. Talk about an emotional roller coaster this morning. “Go downstairs. I’ll be down there faster if all three of you go. Otherwise, I’ll think about doing something else.” Bella wiggled her eyebrows. When understanding dawned, they groaned.

“No teasing, baby. Now is not the time. Tonight, though, we’ll show you what kind of teasing we can do.” Clay leaned down, kissed her, and walked out of the bathroom.

Clint kissed Bella, pulling her body against his. “Don’t take too long, baby. We’ll be waiting for you.” He held on to her longer than necessary, enjoying the feel of her against him.

Cody smacked Bella's bottom before kissing her neck. "Get ready, baby. We'll see you in a few."

They all walked out of the bathroom, closing the door with a soft click. They headed down to talk to their parents, ready to tell them the great news. Bella had agreed to marry them. This was the best day ever.

* * * *

Clint couldn't stop smiling. He had overreacted earlier, and now they were engaged. He was just so happy that he hadn't pushed her away. Just the thought that he could've been the cause made him take a deep breath and swallow around the lump in this throat. Never again would he react without thought. He would always think of Bella and her happiness first. With that thought, he walked into the kitchen to see their parents sitting down at the kitchen table, waiting for them.

"Good morning, boys." Their mom walked over and kissed them all. "After we talked, I just couldn't get here fast enough. Your dad drives too slowly."

"Don't look at me. It was Ryan," their dad Frank said, pointing at their other dad.

Clint shook his head. Their parents were so funny. It was so obvious how much they loved each other, though.

"Tell me all about Bella. She's still here, right? I came as quickly as I could. I want to help you boys." Their mom was so kindhearted, thinking that they needed her help. She continued to think they were little boys instead of men.

"Of course, Momma. She's in the shower. She'll be down soon." Cody hugged his mom.

They wanted to introduce Bella to everyone, and they had some wonderful news to share, but he wanted to wait for Bella before telling his parents.

They chatted about different things that were happening at the ranch, and about their parents' vacation, until Bella walked into the kitchen.

She walked in quietly, not wanting to interrupt, but he noticed her quickly. They all noticed her. Clint, Clay, and Cody turned around and smiled at her. Their mom walked over, holding her arms out, and Bella walked to her, enjoyed a motherly embrace. She felt welcomed to the family instantly. This was going to be her family. The only thing missing was her mom and, of course, Hannah. Thinking about Hannah made her realize that they hadn't spoken for a while. She needed to remember to call her.

"You must be Bella. I'm Paula, but you can call me Mom. It's so wonderful to finally meet you, dear. My boys have told me tons about you." She was a beautiful woman, in her late sixties, with the same brown eyes as her sons, and the same sincere smile. "These are my husbands, Ryan and Frank." She introduced them naturally. It was obvious she loved these men from the sparkle in her eyes and the slight blush on her cheeks.

Bella felt like she was being watched, as if her men weren't sure of her reaction. "It's so wonderful meeting you all. We're having quite a barbecue today. I'm so glad you all are back in town. I can't wait to introduce you to my friends Jessica and Alyssa. They're probably already here."

"Before you go searching outside for your friends, I think we should share our newest announcement," Clint said, pulling Bella toward him and his brothers.

"What news?" his mom asked with a question apparent on her face.

"Bella has agreed to marry us," Clint announced.

Their mom shrieked and started hugging them all, as their dads walked around congratulating them.

"That's great news. Oh my God, there might be babies again soon."

Their mom was so overjoyed by the news that she was already planning grandkids. They hadn't even talked to Bella about that yet. She looked over at them and smiled. She didn't seem upset by the talk about babies.

They all celebrated for a little while, talking about wedding plans. Finally, they walked outside to a bunch of people getting ready for the party to begin. They had an announcement to make soon.

* * * *

Bella saw Jessica and Alyssa pull up in the work truck and walked over to meet them. She had taken a nice shower and gotten dressed in a yellow sundress and flip-flops. She was looking forward to showing her friends her ring. Her hand felt a little heavier, and she kept looking down to see the ring sparkle in the sunlight.

Bella opened the passenger door, letting Jessica out. "It's so good to see you guys."

It had felt like forever since she'd seen them. Alyssa walked around the truck and grabbed her amazing dip from Jessica.

"Look at this place. This is a party. I can't believe all these people are here." Alyssa was obviously a bit shocked. It seemed like the whole town was here, working together to get the ranch ready for an event.

"I know, right? I came out this morning and the place was transformed into this, a dance floor, a bar, and a huge grill."

Bella waited patiently for them to notice the ring, but it wasn't happening. "I got engaged!" she shrieked, waving her hand in front of them.

"What?"

"That's amazing!"

Jessica and Alyssa grabbed her hand and inspected the ring closely.

"It belonged to their grandmother. This morning I told them that

I'm moving here. They proposed after I told them." Bella decided to skip telling them about the misunderstanding. She didn't want to go through an explanation.

"This is incredible. I mean, I knew you had feelings for them, but I didn't expect a ring this soon," Alyssa told her.

She knew Alyssa had known how she was feeling because she had kept giving her looks here and there.

"I'm happy for you. I guess we only need a three-bedroom house now. Since you'll be moving in with your men now." Jessica smiled at her.

"Alyssa and I have been talking about a store name. We want to call it Love Song. What do you think? We went through the list of different boutique names, but since we're having lingerie, artwork, jewelry, and other miscellaneous things, we thought that sounded nice."

Jessica was waiting for Bella to respond. She was so happy, though, that the name of the store really didn't matter. She had her men, her friends, and a new store. Nothing could be better.

"I think it's great. Love Song it is. I also wanted you both to know that I'm going to call Hannah. I think her jewelry would be perfect for the store. I hope she'll come out here. Although, she's overly cautious, so I don't know."

"Cautious? She's a bit paranoid, Bella. You're right, though, I think it would be better if she came here. She doesn't have anyone else," Jessica told her with a small shake of her head and a grin. It was great to have friends like Jessica and Alyssa, who were always on board with everything.

They all walked toward the other people sitting by the picnic tables. Bella smiled at her men. Clint was manning the grill, with Chase and Beau helping him. Clay was in charge of the music. He was playing country while talking to his dads. Cody was behind the bar, with Justin and Grant, helping hand out ice-cold beers. She made eye contact with each of them as she walked with Jessica and Alyssa.

She smiled and flew kisses their way. This was the relationship she had always wanted, that she had searched for all her adult life. It was amazing. She never knew that taking a road trip would lead her to her future.

Clint handed off the grilling job to Chase and Beau and walked over to her. "You look happy, baby." Clint pulled Bella close to him and leaned down to nuzzle her neck.

"I love you." She held him tight, stepping on her tiptoes, and kissed his lips.

"I love you, too, baby." Clint kissed her back. He took her hand and took her around to introduce her to everyone, this time as their future wife.

The music was going, and people were enjoying the atmosphere, playing horseshoes, dancing, eating good food, and having some beers. It was an experience most people never had, the sense of community. All the people here were friends. It just seemed so surreal, and Bella had never experienced anything like it before.

* * * *

As the party wound down hours later, people slowly started to leave, and the evening got darker. Bella yawned, realizing how truly tired she was. She stretched, rubbing her eyes. Being outside all day in the sun had worn her out.

Clay came up behind her and put his arms around her. "Tired, baby?" He pulled her close, and she relaxed her body against his. "Let's go inside and take a nice, relaxing bath. I want to hold you." Clay kissed her neck and gently bit her exposed shoulder.

"Mmmmm…that sounds heavenly." Bella felt herself grow wetter when he bit into her shoulder. She was starting to wake up. Being close to any of her men had her juices flowing. Bella rubbed her legs together to help ease the ache that had started.

"Come on, baby. Clint and Cody are watching us. I know they

want to join us in the huge tub," he told her, taking her hand and leading her toward the house and the waiting bathroom. It had been a taxing day, full of fun, making a huge announcement to their friends. Of course, everyone was happy for them, but many of the men, who were also searching for the one they could share, were envious.

Hearing about Bella, Alyssa, and Jessica's new business, Love Song, people were curious. A store full of sexy lingerie, artwork, and sex toys was going to be quite popular. With more women coming to town, everything was looking up, so maybe the envious looks wouldn't last too long.

Clint and Cody followed closely behind Clay and Bella as they made their way into the house. Clay walked straight into the bathroom and started moving his hands up and down her body. He started to undress her as Bella, in turn, started stripping him. It was obvious that they were both running out of patience, and they started moving faster.

Clint came into the bathroom, started the bathwater, added some Epsom salts, and started undressing as he watched Bella being stripped by his brother. When he reached for his zipper, he was staring at Bella's creamy breasts. His mouth began to water, and he licked his lips. He walked up behind Bella, wrapped his arms around her, and pumped his hard cock into the crevice of her sexy ass.

Clay cupped Bella's breasts, weighing them in his hands. Using his thumb and forefinger, he pinched her nipples until hearing Bella moan. Clay cupped and kneaded, flicking his thumbs across her hard nipples, arousing them further.

Cody watched the scene play out in front of him. Clint was holding Bella tight against his chest, kissing her neck and nibbling her shoulders. Clay was paying close attention to Bella's breasts. She was moaning and moving, desperate for more, silently begging them.

"Tell us what you want, baby," he whispered to her. "What do you want us to do to your body, sweetheart?" Cody watched her. His words always had an effect on her.

"I need more! I want to be fucked!" Bella yelled. She was pushing her ass into Clint's cock, and her pussy into Clay's. Yeah, their baby needed some cock.

"Get in the tub, baby. Clint and Clay will take care of you." Cody helped Bella into the tub as his brothers got in as well. "Clay, sit down. Bella needs your cock in her pussy."

Clay grinned at him and sat down. Bella went to him, ready to impale herself on his cock.

Clay slid his hands down her waist and held her steady as he watched her rise up on her knees, then groaned as she sank down his rigid length. Bella started riding him with quick, fast strokes. Her goal was obvious. She wanted to come, and she rode him, not caring about anything else around her.

Cody's voice broke through the haze that Clay found himself in. "Clay, stop her so that Clint can get in that ass."

Clay grabbed Bella's hips, taking the control back. He stopped her movements and ravaged her mouth.

Bella kissed Clay with complete abandon. Their teeth banged together, but that didn't slow her down. When Bella felt a finger pushing into her ass, she slowed the kissing down and started to relax a little, wanting Clint to fuck her. She started panting, enjoying the full feeling of having Clay buried in her pussy and Clint's fingers stretching her ass.

"All right, baby, looks like Clint's ready to take that sexy ass. I want you to take a deep breath, push back, and keep those muscles relaxed." This was Cody's show. He told everyone what to do and when to do it. This was turning him on. His cock was hard as stone, begging for release.

Bella waited for Clint, but he took his time, rubbing her hips and ass. "Damn it, take me." She was losing her patience.

"Slap her ass, Clint, and then fuck her hard. Our baby is horny."

Clint did exactly what Cody told him to do. He spanked her ass, which had her moaning and moving on top of Clay. Clint grabbed

Bella's hip with one hand and guided his cock into her dark hole with the other. He wanted to take things gently, but Bella wasn't in the mood for slow. She shoved her ass at him, and he slipped in deeper.

"Oh, fuck, baby! I'm not gonna last. Take it slower." Clint was trying to slow her down, but gave up, giving her what she craved. He sank deeply inside her luscious little body. Bella bucked and moved until finally breaking their already strained control. Clint and Clay started moving.

Bella was being pushed and pulled between Clint and Clay. She felt sexy and desired.

"How do you feel, baby? Do you like being packed full of cock?" Cody leaned closer to the tub and talked dirty to Bella. He knew that it made her crazier.

"Cody…I need your cock. Pull it out for me," she told him. She licked her lips and watched Cody stand and start taking off his jeans. She stared at his hand as he lowered the zipper, waiting to see his cock appear. When his large, hard cock sprang free, she moaned. "Come closer, Cody. I want to suck your cock." Bella leaned over the edge of the tub, letting Clint and Clay take over while she focused some attention on Cody.

She moaned deep in her throat when his spicy taste hit her tongue. She started kissing and sucking the spongy head into her mouth. She used her teeth, gently biting, not hard enough to hurt, just trying to get his attention. Cody put his hand in her hair and held tightly. She loved that feeling of being controlled, and right now, her men were controlling her body.

"She's so damn wet. I can feel her muscles pulsing. Damn…fuck her into me harder, Clint. She's close."

They all worked together, taking Bella to the edge. She sucked Cody harder and harder.

"Oh, baby, your mouth feels so good on my cock. If you don't want me coming in that pretty mouth, you better let go," Cody warned her. It only took another minute. "I'm coming, baby. Oh fuck, don't stop."

Cody pumped his hips, shoving his cock down her throat. She swallowed around his shaft as jets of cum spurted out of his cock. Cody came hard and groaned loud. Bella licked his cock clean as he rubbed her head. He leaned down and kissed her, enjoying their connection.

Bella groaned as Clint and Clay played havoc on her body.

"Clay, reach down to her clit and make her come." Cody told him as he watched his brothers pleasure their woman.

Clay rubbed her clit and felt Bella's muscles clench his cock. He was close as well. He started kissing Bella, eating at her lips, enjoying her taste and having her in his arms.

Clay felt her start to come before he heard her. Her body quivered with spasms so hard he was glad he was holding her.

She cried out and yelled loudly, "Oh God! Oh God!" She kept moving until she collapsed against Clay's chest, trying to regain her breathing and heartbeat. Every time with them was an explosion. She saw stars, and she shook uncontrollably, multiple orgasms at one time. Unbelievable.

* * * *

Clay held Bella. Both Clint and Cody soaped up their hands. They all took care of her. They worked together, bringing her down, soothing her, cleaning her up, and getting her ready for bed. Clay seemed to be the lucky one. He was able to hold her and kiss her. He knew Bella was completely relaxed. Her breathing changed. She fell asleep in his arms. He smiled at his brothers.

"She fell asleep," he whispered, looking down at the woman who had forever changed their lives for the better. He was finally at a point in his life where he felt at ease.

Cody smiled. "She's so perfect for us. I'm just glad we found her."

“Me too,” Clint agreed. “I’ll get out first, dry off, and then we can all help get Bella dried off and into bed.”

Clint climbed out and dried off quickly. Cody climbed out as well, and they helped Clay to stand and then took Bella out of his arms. Together they dried her off and then put her in bed. Clint and Cody climbed into the bed, each taking a side, while Clay put his head on Bella’s thigh. They would always be together, her being at the center of their world.

Bella moved around until she was comfortable, held tight in Clint and Cody’s arms. She was facing Clint and gently kissed his chest while pushing her bottom into Cody’s groin, trying to find the perfect spot. “Mmmm…I love you guys. Good night.”

“Good night, baby.” Clint kissed the top of her head.

“Good night, sweetie.” Cody rubbed her bottom, leaning down and kissing the back of her neck.

“Sweet dreams.” Clay rubbed her thigh over the blanket.

The road trip was the best decision Bella had ever made. The next step was getting Hannah here. Just maybe everyone she loved would find their happily ever after, or at least a new beginning with love.

# THE END

**WWW.ALICIAWHITEBOOKS.COM**

# ABOUT THE AUTHOR

Writing has been a dream come true for Alicia White. She started out losing her job and looking for work in the criminal-justice field. With a push from her husband, she submitted this book to Siren Publishing. Now she spends her time volunteering with a child's-rights activist group, helping her daughter with homework, and spending time with her family.

## *Also by Alicia White*

Ménage Amour: Journey of a Thousand Miles 2:
*Handcuffs for Hannah*

Available at
**BOOKSTRAND.COM**

Siren Publishing, Inc.
www.SirenPublishing.com

CPSIA information can be obtained at www.ICGtesting.com
Printed in the USA
LVOW071410160212

269014LV00007B/58/P

9 781619 266414